The Tattered Box

Paul Schumacher

Cover photos by Bill and Arlis Kuess.

Cover designed by Chris Rackley, www.chrisrackley.com.

Author photo by Gail Schumacher.

For Bill, the greatest storyteller
I ever met

Contents

Acknowledgments

Like all great endeavors, this novel was in no way the work of one. Thanks to numerous friends and family members who reviewed my manuscript and provided helpful feedback and encouragement. I'm sure I'm forgetting someone, but here it goes: Brad Cook, Dan Landgraf, Dean Book, Mary Ellen Tonsing, Scott Jonas, Chris Rackley, all of my critique group, and too many Schumachers to name. Thanks also to Aviva Layton and Rachel Weaver for their professional editing skills.

Thanks to my father for his knowledge in the history of Watertown, Wisconsin (of which Waterville is based), and to my mother for her editing skills, support, and kind words. Thanks to Uncle Tom for his passion in English and tolerance in applying it to me and my writing. Thanks also to Chris Rackley for lending his amazing artistic talents to convert this story into a book cover.

Special thanks to my father-in-law, Bill, for without him this novel would have never existed. You lived, told, and re-told so many wonderful stories, I simply had to write this novel. The world needed to hear what I already knew. We love you and miss you dearly.

Of course, the last here are really the first, thanks to my amazing wife and children who not only put up with me, but also love and encourage me to pursue my passion for writing. For all of you, I am eternally grateful.

"Sharing tales of those we've lost is how we keep from really losing them."
— Mitch Albom, *For One More Day*

Chapter 1

My grandpa struggled to walk down the dimly lit hallway, leaning against the wall with every step. I could hear his hobbled gait from all the way in the kitchen, so I anticipated his arrival. I still admire that hall. Rows of pictures and family portraits decorated its walls, many from happier times. I never did check if the pictures were ordered chronologically, but a stroll down that hall might have transported me to somewhere I never intended.

He meandered toward the kitchen, cradling something under an arm. A piece of food fell from his shirt, and for a split second, I thought he'd fall if he stepped on it. He maneuvered around it, surprising for a man whose belly had blocked any chance of seeing his feet.

When he finally arrived, he placed a small, peculiar box on the table right next to my Calculus book. The box was timeworn and resembled a long-lost treasure chest. It was many shades of dirty brown, and the varnish had fallen off in a number of places. The musty smell was of a rarely opened attic, and it had a curved top like a prop from an old pirate movie. A small, tarnished lock kept the cover secured, even though the weak, rusty hinges could easily be broken.

I put down my pencil and decided Newton would have to wait until later.

"What's that, Grandpa?" I asked.

My grandpa lived down that hall ever since I was eight. He mostly kept to himself, but coffee or ice cream could bait him any time of the day. His weathered face and deep eyes were signs of an extended past, a past he was more than willing to tell me about. My mom gave him his old standby crew cut every few weeks, and I swore his nose had grown over the years. Probably from all his storytelling.

"Well..." he hesitated. "It's a box I thought you'd like to have."

"Depends what's in it." I leaned back and shrugged my shoulders.

"Items I've collected over the years. Important stuff."

I stared at it and wondered what could possibly mean so much to him, a man who hadn't left the house in a decade. My imagination pranced around a field of possibilities as I yearned for anything that could bring me the fame and fortune I needed to get out of this place. Hundred-year-old gold coins, vintage Italian watches, or a Colt 45 owned by Billy the Kid. Anything.

"Now hold on a minute, Stallion. Where'd I put that damn key?" He leaned to his right and pushed his arm onto the table, exhaling a forceful grunt.

He dug around in the left pocket of his raggedy, blue pants. I always envisioned he had a closet full of identical pants with the same holes and rips in them, but I guess that wasn't the case. He finally found the key and slipped it out of his pocket. It was shinier than I expected, although maybe it was reflecting my newly minted enthusiasm.

"I've kept this in a safe place waiting for just the right time," he revealed with heavy breath. "I don't remember much, but I do remember where I kept this."

He straightened his back and handed me the key.

I snatched it out of his hand and momentarily fumbled with it. The key was unlike anything I had ever seen. With sharp teeth at one end and a long, twisted neck, I swore the intertwining, circular handle was a cursive script trying to tell me something. But I was too preoccupied with opening the chest to find my treasure trove.

I applied the key to the rusty lock.

I slowly pushed back the cover and rested it on its hinges. It emitted a sustained creaking noise like the basement door of a haunted house. My eyes danced from one item to the next. Touching, shifting, hoping that something was hiding. But I quickly realized I had seen them all.

"What the hell is this?"

"Watch your mouth, young man! There's no reason to speak that way. These items mean a hell of a lot to me."

I collapsed into my chair with folded arms and emanated a deep moan. "Ok, then. Tell me about them. I'm dying to hear…"

He reached in to grab something, his hand noticeably shaking. It was like the beginning of a magic trick where I guessed the ploy even before it started. He pulled out a baseball. The caked dirt had accumulated long before yesterday with scuff marks all around its surface. I could barely make out the seams.

"Is that from the game in '41 you always tell me about?" I tilted my head and pointed to it.

"Sure is, John. Nice to know you actually listen."

He adjusted himself in his chair, took a sip of his lukewarm coffee, then cleared his throat with three successive spurts. With the inevitable momentum building, I plopped my calculator next to my notebook, hoping his eyesight wasn't good enough to see my reaction.

"Let me tell ya about it…" The man never met a story he didn't love.

I took a swig of my Mountain Dew and wished my mom would come home soon. Man, was I hungry. I glanced around the room, not really focusing on anything. What was I thinking giving him a cue? I've heard all his stories before. My math homework had a loud, thunderous heartbeat, my upcoming baseball game loomed large, and the last thing I had time for was another story.

"So back in the spring of '41, I played for those Goslings of yours. Waterville was a different town back then, but we were a darn good ball club. You should have seen Frank McKenna play third. Had an arm like a pistol and was faster than any deer up north. You know Frank?"

"Grandpa, that was like 60 years ago. Sorry, don't know him."

I always found his questions annoying yet amusing. They don't make much sense, but he does have his ulterior motives. If he's going to talk, it certainly helps if someone listens. I remember one time I watched my mom fall asleep during a rare story about the war. My sister, Sarah, and I were peeking around the corner, covering our mouths to muffle our laughter. We were supposed to be in bed.

"Oh, yeah, you probably wouldn't," he continued. "So we're tied 4-4 in the bottom of the last inning. It was crappy weather, but what do you expect for mid-April? The manager from Hartland insisted we wait till the weather cleared, but ol' Mr. Kohl, the ump, would hear nothing of it. 'Let's play ball' he bellowed louder than a shotgun in the woods.

"Yours truly was up to bat. Their pitcher stared me down like a hungry dog, but I just smiled back."

My grandpa flashed me a sly, knowing grin. He either had twitches from all that coffee he drank, or he just winked at me.

"First pitch, right down the pipe. I saw it coming, but the best that stinging bat could do was a slow dribbler to short. When Pee Wee started bobbling that ball, I was off to the pig races. As I reached first, I started thinking, 'Man, whatcha doing in the middle of the bag? Get outta my way.'

"As fast as I could trot in the slop, I ran right smack into the first baseman. The ball popped out of his glove and spurted into the outfield, so I headed for second. I jumped over the guy sprawled on the ground, then slid in knocking over their second baseman, too. Who knew where the ball ended up? So I took off for third.

"The shortstop knew to get the heck out of my way, but their third baseman looked wide-eyed and downright terrified as I slid into third. He was right behind the bag so I splattered him with mud. Ball was free and rolled out into the outfield.

"I headed for home. Sure enough, their catcher was blocking the plate. Not sure if he was blind or hadn't been paying attention. I made one dramatic dive into home, starting my slide halfway from third. Collided with that bugger, too.

"Oddest home run you'll ever see. My teammates came runnin' out celebrating our win like a bunch of wild, screamin' girls. 'Course, that Hartland team picked themselves up out of the mud and barreled in like the cavalry. Ol' Mr. Kohl called it a win for Waterville and told those Hartland folks to calm down and back off. 'You were all in the baseline and deserved to be knocked over,' he tells 'em. Man, what a game!"

He leaned forward, grinned a hearty grin, then almost knocked over his coffee with his swinging, clenched fist.

"Great story, Grandpa," I responded with a subdued excitement. He certainly weaved pretty good tales, but to me, the embellishments siphoned all credibility from his stories. A home run in the mud? Seriously? I've often considered looking it up on the microfilm at the library, but that would admit that I cared.

If only he discovered a different story now and then. If only he experienced something new. Not sure where he would have gotten it from, to be honest. Like a man thrown into prison until he paid his debt, he was an aging man trapped in a life of nothingness.

"Did you ever meet up with those Hartland guys again?" I envisioned a wanted poster hanging from every tree in Hartland with a picture of the old guy wearing his muddy, pinstriped uniform, holding a bat over his shoulder, and sporting a Snidely Whiplash mustache. No wonder I laughed.

"Yeah, we played 'em in a scrimmage nine months later. We all thought it was hilarious. Best day of your life doesn't have to be the worst of somebody else's, even if you wind up getting knocked on your ass."

His eloquence was only preceded by his good looks, which wasn't saying much. Good thing he never decided to write fortune cookies.

"So… how'd you get that dirty, old ball then?" I glanced at it resting in his hand.

"I left that game so excited I plumb forgot to grab the game ball. When you win a game like that, you've gotta get the game ball, kid. 'Course, I was also soaked to my skivvies by that point and frankly just wanted to get home."

"Then… how'd you get it?"

"Well, it was my good friend Eddy. He grabbed the ball from the ump and threw it in his bag. Next day at school, he flipped it to me and said, 'Hey, I thought you should have this.' As you can tell, it was obvious which ball it was. What a pal."

"That's awesome he kept it for ya."

I leaned forward, grabbed the ball from him, then held it in my dirtied hand. The ball was smaller and heavier than I was used to, and the leather felt harsh and rough. As I rubbed it, some of the dirt scattered onto the floor and tabletop.

For the first time in my life, I actually considered the slight possibility that he told the truth with that story of his. Minus all the embellishments, of course.

"You think about having your teammates sign it?"

"Not really. We'd have to clean it then. Kinda nice to have it dirty. Reminds me of the game and what made it so special."

I offered the ball back to my grandpa, and he cradled it with his shaky hand. He gazed at it with an intensity I hadn't seen from him in a long time. More dirt fell off as he attempted to grasp it. His hand was not as nimble as it used to be, but he applied a surprisingly tight grip. With as steady a hand as he could muster, two fingers bent just enough for me to recognize what he was doing. His fingernails dug into the ball right against the seams.

"I didn't know you threw a knuckleball."

"Yeah, did for a bit. A good friend taught me how. I didn't use it much, though. Wasn't the most popular pitch in my days, but it sure was fun to throw."

Six months earlier, I taught myself how to throw a knuckleball. Rain or shine I threw it until I mastered the skill.

Our garage door never looked the same after that. I still remember how I couldn't wait to throw my intimidating knuckler in a game that year.

I shifted my focus to the other contents of the box, viewing the items like I thought they'd start moving. Each was small enough to be held in one hand but large enough for me to find them. A delicate ring hid in the corner. I set it on the table as it reflected what little sunlight seeped through the kitchen window.

Next to it, I placed the white feather, making sure it didn't touch the scraps of dirt scattered on the table. The toothpick felt so brittle and frail. I was certain it would break as I inspected it in my hand. While my grandpa focused intently on the ball, out of the corner of my eye I saw him grin as I positioned the toothpick on the table.

The ticket was about the same length as the toothpick with a similar dull, brown color. I placed it next to the toothpick. Again, I watched for my grandpa's reaction. He gazed at the ticket in such a slow, soft manner, I knew he was thinking of something else.

The grey, wool mitten induced no reaction whatsoever, almost like he was trying to avoid it. I watched him closely as I brought out the small, pocket-sized Bible. He stared at it as I placed it on the table.

I sat back and waited for drawn-out stories about each item. But they never came. It was the first time I ever saw him miss an opportunity like that. Looking back on it, I think he figured time and experience would be the best storytellers. Somehow he knew.

The noise at the front door startled me. Keys dropped on the stand in the foyer, as my sister came running around the corner.

"What's that? How cool." Sarah ran over and draped her arms on Grandpa's shoulders.

"It's from a long, long time ago."

She slipped on the dirty floor as she stepped around him to get a better look.

It was pretty easy to tell when my mom entered.

"What in the blazes happened here? You boys have got to clean up that table right away. John, you've gotta finish your homework 'cause you need to be at your game in an hour. And you'd better wear something warm and waterproof 'cause there's a front coming in tonight. It's gonna be a cold one."

Instant lecture in a can. Just add water.

"Yeah, yeah Mom. Did Grandpa show you his baseball?"

"How'd it get so dirty?"

"It's from that game in '41," I attempted to jog her memory.

"The one where he knocked over the whole darn team and won the game? Course I remember. Interesting box, too, Dad. I'd love to see it, but we really have to get ready for John's game tonight. Clean up that table pronto so we can eat."

He angled toward the box and leaned his arms on the table. The lid closed with the same haunted, creaky sound, only this time in reverse. He glanced at it one last time, then handed it to me. The ball thudded against the side. I sensed a grin hiding behind a teeth-tightening wince – that is, if he had any teeth – as he outstretched his shoulder.

"Thanks, Grandpa. This is... an interesting gift."

He looked down, took a long, deep breath, then scooped the dirt from the table with his hands. He stared at it, deciding what to do with scraps of earth that came from a different time.

He clearly sensed my apprehension about the box. I couldn't help but think I was just handed a nice parting gift. Like I had just lost miserably at a game show, but they didn't want me to go home empty-handed. Of course, I might have been happier if I simply lowered my expectations, but that's easier said than done.

I packed up the box and decided I wanted to sift through it after my game that night. Maybe I'd find something interesting. I took it in the garage and decided to drop it in my baseball bag.

Even now, ten years later, I cannot explain why I decided to do that. But I did. And honestly, it turned out to be one of the most rewarding things I'd ever done in my God-given life.

I headed back to the kitchen and swept the dirt off the floor. Pieces crumbled into the dustpan. My mom and Grandpa were engaged in a lively conversation about fishing.

My mom had never picked up a reel in her life, and my grandpa hadn't fished since Nixon claimed he wasn't a crook. But somehow the topic came up now and then.

"You'd better get ready, John. Don't forget, it's gonna be a cold one," my mom reminded me.

"Don't freeze your butt off, Johnny boy," my grandpa chimed in.

I headed to my room to change. As I put on my uniform, I glanced out the window. The rain had started to fall.

Chapter 2

"Mom, let's go!" I shouted from the foyer. As if the sound of my cleats hitting the linoleum didn't give it away. I shuddered at the thought of her driving me to my game – I was 18, after all – but she said she needed the car.

"Coming dear," interrupting her lively, post-dinner conversation with my grandpa. This time, they were discussing the therapeutic elements of bowling, or something like that.

I finished lacing up when Sarah came running up to give me a hug. It was a ritual before every one of my games, from Little League up through high school.

She was a freshman and had caught up to Mom in height. She was also a spitting image of our jerk of a father: dark brown eyes, dirty blond hair that would only look good on a surfer, and this annoying way of smiling at everything.

"You comin' to watch, Sarah?" I asked.

"Are ya kiddin' me? It's colder than a polar bear's pajamas out there."

I laughed. I did always find her funny. She'd also make friends with a flower if she didn't think the other flowers in the field would be jealous. She was the most thoughtful, compassionate person I'd ever met. To a fault, in my opinion. Her buttery softheartedness was enough to drive a cynic like me over the edge.

"You're telling me. I'm not even sure we're gonna play tonight. If we do, I'll toss ya my uniform when I get back. I'll even sign it."

"Ooh, then it'd be all wet and muddy. Ah, no thanks." She grimaced then gave me a playful shove. It was the first time I had seen her smile since she got braces the week before.

"Mom! Are ya coming or not?" I glared into the kitchen, leaning around my sister. I hated to be late, especially for a ballgame.

"I'm coming. I'm coming," she mumbled as she entered the foyer to grab her keys.

We headed out the side door and dashed toward the garage. I never saw the value in having a detached garage, especially with the lousy weather we get in Wisconsin. They were clearly heartier folks back in the 1920's when that house was built.

"It's really cold out here, John. You sure you're gonna play?" She angled her head back as she eased the car out of the compact garage.

"Coach really wants to get the game in. Caleb told me he's gonna wear five layers of shirts out there."

"Sounds like a good idea." She turned the corner onto Main.

"Who's at the grocery store tonight?"

"Hank's covering for me. I originally hoped to go watch your game, but now I'm not so sure. Afraid I'll catch a cold. Mind if I stay home and get some laundry done? I need to run to the store, too."

"No problem. I'm guessing no one else will be there, anyway."

She made a left onto Francis, heading toward the ball field. I spotted the river just beyond the field, but the cliff by the river's edge appeared to rise into an endless cloud. A thick fog had rolled in as the former high school beyond the river was only there in my imagination.

"Say, what was that box you and Grandpa were poring over?"

"A gift for me, apparently. He grabbed it out of his room, and we were sortin' through it when you and Sarah walked in."

"Anything interesting?"

"I know you loved the dirt."

She gave me a quick glance with a noticeable scowl.

"Other than that," I continued, "not much, really. Seemed like this collection of random junk he picked up off the ground over the years. Everything was either small and pointless or old and dirty. Why he gave 'em to me, I'll never know."

"Well, you know him. He's got a story behind each one."

She eased into the last parking spot near the ball field, trying to avoid getting wedged between two gigantic Chevy trucks.

"Yeah, no kidding." I glanced out the rain-streaked window. "I thought it'd be, I don't know, worth something. Then I'd buy us a bigger house, Dad would come back, the choir would sing, the elves and fairies would show up. You know, all the believable crap in this world."

She closed her eyes and rubbed the agitation off her forehead. It was always the same uneasiness every time I mentioned my father, and my layers of sarcasm didn't help. She opened her eyes, stretched her arm across the backrest, then slanted toward me. I leaned back against the passenger door.

"John, there's nothing wrong with dreaming of a better life," she sighed. "But don't let it get in the way of enjoying what you have. I know I've told you this before, but I'm sorry. Your father's not coming back. I don't even know where he is. I love our house, I love our life, and I especially love you guys. Your grandpa also adores you and enjoys spending time with you."

The windows started to fog up, creating an eerie sense of isolation. Things felt smaller, closer, but not necessarily in a good way.

"I just wish his stories wouldn't drag on so darn long." I slapped my knee with my glove. "I've heard 'em all before. I wish he gave Cliff Notes versions now and then."

Of course, these conversations always popped up right before I had to go somewhere.

"You'll appreciate 'em at some point, John. You will," she reassured me. "You should head over. Looks like your whole team's warming up."

We both wiped condensation off the front window, just enough so we could see down the third baseline. She was right. I was the last one there.

"Yup, gotta run. Let's chat when I get back."

"Sounds good. Have a great game, honey. Stay warm!"

Knowing my team was busy practicing, I leaned over to give her a quick peck on the cheek. I grabbed my bag from the backseat and headed over to practice.

"Hey Caleb, what's up?" I said.

"Nice of you to join us..." he mumbled. He was a stickler for time so his annoyance didn't surprise me.

I started throwing with my buddy.

We've known each other since third grade, but we didn't become good friends until we played ball together. He was always the best kid on the team. Everyone knew it, even him. But he tried not to show it, at least with me.

My grandpa said Caleb reminded him of Mickey Mantle. Partly because he was a power-hitting outfielder, but the good looks and farm boy physique certainly helped. Sarah hid in her room whenever he'd come over. An embarrassing crush will do that to a girl.

"This is gonna be a fun one. Love the weather." I threw him the ball.

"Oh, it's gonna be a blast!" Caleb outstretched his glove and pointed to the muddy ground. "I'll be sure to dive for some out there. Been a while since I've done a Slip 'N Slide."

"Considering how much you weigh, you'll slide all the way to the infield. Just stay away from short. I don't wanna get trampled out there."

"Ya wimp. I'll be sure to yell before I run into ya."

"Gee thanks."

My hands were numb, but I was proud I could take any weather that came my way. My mom never understood why I wore shorts and a T-shirt, even in winter. I'd tell her I didn't have to worry about the weather since I always knew what to wear.

"Ok, boys, let's get started!" yelled my coach, Mr. Finch.

He was a bald, burly man with a large head and even larger face. Everything about him was big. We used to joke that baseballs would get lost in his hands, never to be seen or heard from again. I think God created him specifically to be a coach. I heard when he was little, he'd sit in the stands and yell at ball players to tell 'em what to do. Doesn't surprise me.

As I headed to the dugout, I oddly thought of an item from the box: the ring. I was going to ask Mom if that was Grandma's ring, but I remembered she wore hers at her funeral. How could I forget the ring on her left hand, reflecting the bright lights on an otherwise dreary day?

The physically ill feeling was not something I easily forgot, just hurting inside for the loss my grandpa felt. First time I saw him truly angry. Sure, he had bouts of grumpiness, but this was different. His weary face portrayed such a deep exhaustion and sadness I hadn't seen before.

The rain came down harder, but we were determined to get the game in. Mr. Finch said we didn't have an opening on our schedule for a make-up game.

The first inning went well. Caleb drove me in with a double to left, and we took the lead 1-0. I had gotten on base by smacking a liner at their second baseman whom I didn't like very much, even back to Little League days. He fell on his butt trying to catch it, slipping on a field that got worse by the minute. Served him right, the yellow-bellied trash talker.

They took the lead in the fourth. Their catcher hit one up the middle that our pitcher, Josh, barely missed. So did I. Normally I'm pretty fast, but those were the toughest conditions I had ever played in. Caleb hustled in from center and tried to catch the guy at the plate, but he lost his grip on the ball as it sailed over the backstop and almost hit the ump's car.

By the top of the fifth, we were sludging about in one gigantic mud puddle. Just about any contact became a hit, so it unraveled into a contest against the elements more than anything else. Tied 3-3, even I was getting cold. I danced around, attempting to shake the wetness from my uniform. I yanked off my glove and rubbed my hand down the side of my leg.

What little crowd we had at the start - Caleb's brother and a few hearty Rotary Club members who attend our games - had all since left for drier, warmer surroundings.

Their slugger was still unhappy about a close play at third. He argued with the ump, but the ump would hear nothing of it. His retaliation was to swing for the fence. On a 2-1 fastball, Josh threw one right down the middle of the plate. The guy swung with everything he had in him and made perfect contact. I can still hear the vibrations and echoes of that hit.

I got a good read on it and made three quick strides to my left. I was bound and determined to catch one up the middle. I saw it coming. My glove was up. I had it.

My memory faded considerably from there on out, though. I have heard a life-altering event tends to happen in slow motion. It still does. But the force of the ball against my right temple certainly muddled my memory.

I don't remember hitting the ground very hard. I do recall hearing many voices coming from right above me. The raindrops struck my face with an unwelcome force. Odd since I was knocked out cold.

Above all the other voices and commotion, I distinctly heard Caleb telling me it was going to be alright. The wavering in his voice scared me more than anything, but I couldn't find a way to express it.

Not that anyone would have listened.

Chapter 3

A cold rush pressed hard on my chest. I gasped for air. What was I to do? I was desperate. I needed to breathe. Confusion and lack of control were daunting enemies. I wrestled with them, only making matters worse.

It was a curious mix of sensations. The hastening movement overwhelmed me, while the alternating periods of restful slowness were somehow reassuring. I lay lifeless on that field, never moving. Or was I? Everything flashed by like I was driving into an unrelenting snowstorm. My hands formed a firm grip, providing a false impression of control.

My thoughts and memories were a jumbled mess. Some real, some imposters. I had left somewhere, yet I was not entirely sure where I was going. Come to think of it, maybe I didn't recall what happened. Like our vacation to Florida when I was young. Was my memory served by looking at the pictures or did I recall the actual events? In the end, it didn't really matter.

I remember the calming voice above me continued. It was good to know that Caleb was there for me. His friendship meant a lot to me and still does today. But suddenly his voice sounded different yet oddly familiar. Other sounds reverberated off the walls of a hidden chamber, while others became soft and low like the murmuring of a woodwind instrument. I often possess an overactive mind, but this situation raced beyond anything I could have envisioned.

The rain slapped me in the face, dropping out of nowhere from an infinite sky. Maybe they hit me elsewhere, but the feelings I recall are raindrops landing all over my cheeks and forehead. Yet, because of the circumstances, they did have a repetitive calmness that encouraged me to sleep.

I wondered why all those people just stood there and couldn't cover me to keep that stupid rain away. Dammit, I was cold. And annoyed. They clearly ignored my yelling.

* * *

I instinctively reached up and touched my head to stop the throbbing pain. The large, protruding bump that I felt didn't surprise me. A nasty headache distorted my vision, so my eyes fluttered to see where I was. As I straightened myself on the shiny metal bench, I uttered a groan reminiscent of my grandpa.

I looked around for a mirror but didn't see one. I wanted to confirm if I looked as bad as I felt. Where was I anyway? Everything appeared normal and recognizable, yet starkly different. It resembled our home dugout at Riverside, but something wasn't right. It was smaller than I remembered and the benches were a lot shinier. Somebody finally got around to cleaning up that shoddy place.

I gazed at the field through the chain link fence. The slits provided a much needed context. My eyes squinted to help me focus but only narrowed my vision. I could vaguely make out my teammates playing in what resembled one big mud puddle. A mix of rain, fog, and throbbing pain blurred my eyesight, but it was reassuring to see Caleb out in center. Or so I thought. It didn't look like Josh was pitching, though, so Coach must have pulled him.

I spotted a husky man on the opposite end of the dugout. He wore a familiar, off-white uniform with a healthy splattering of mud near the bottom of his legs.

"Hey, Coach! Who's out there pitching?" I asked.

He glanced at me, gave an acknowledging smile, then tipped his cap.

"John! Nice of you to join us."

I heard that before. I squinted and glared at the guy. He didn't look at all familiar to me, and his voice didn't sound like the coach I knew. Something wasn't right.

I leaned forward against the fence and attempted to pull myself up. It surprised me how difficult it was to move. My right hand slid into an opening in the fence to provide some leverage, but I was no match for myself. I instantly crumpled to the ground with a thud.

Coach strutted over and grabbed my arm to help me up. He looked at me with a genuine look of concern that was somehow more intimidating than reassuring.

"Whoa, you need to rest there, kid. You were hit hard by that liner. We almost took you to the hospital but thought we'd wait to see how you're doin'."

Hit hard? You're telling me. That ball must have clobbered the reality out of me, because he didn't look at all like Mr. Finch. Similar uniform, same bulky, freight-train build. But the big nose, pointy chin, and dark brown leathery shoes instantly convinced me he was not my coach.

Everything I thought I knew came into question. I was fighting with myself, but I sure didn't feel like I was winning.

"Where's Mr. Finch?" I slowly removed my cap and scratched the top of my head.

"Not sure I know who you mean, boy. Why don't you just lie down here and get some rest."

He eased me onto the bench with complete care and concern while simultaneously yelling at the top of his lungs, "Hey Frank, move right three steps! This guy's a dead pull hitter!"

He wasn't Mr. Finch, but he sure was a coach. I hoped Frank listened to him, because Coach's yelling sure wasn't helping my throbbing head.

Then I realized, there wasn't a Frank on my team.

"Nice play, Frank!" he yelled, unfortunately a bit too close to my ear. I briefly closed my eyes.

It was prophetic on his part, I had to admit. Hard hit grounder down the third base line. Frank, whoever he was, snagged it and threw him out by a step. Out number three.

They all came running into the dugout, swinging around the edge of the fence and tossing their gloves to the ground. Mud splattered everywhere, giving me a not-so-gentle reminder that it was pouring buckets out there.

They patted me on the back, telling me it was great to see I was awake. I lifted my head to say 'thanks' and glanced at each player as they walked past.

Unfortunately, I had no idea who any of these guys were.

"Let's go! Pull this one out," they encouraged each other with a team-spirited fervor that thankfully rang of familiarity. The entire team stood by the fence, yelling as loudly as they could. I decided to join 'em.

"What's the score?" I nudged the lanky guy next to me who looked like he had just been doused by a pail of water.

He shot me a look like I had just arrived from another planet. "Don't you know? Huh, maybe you wouldn't. It's tied 4-4. Bottom of the seventh."

I considered closing my eyes but couldn't. I had to watch. I rooted and hollered just like everyone else, hoping that no one would decipher my utter daze and bewilderment. No one wants to be the first to ask a question. Doesn't everyone else know what's going on?

But as the last inning progressed, I couldn't believe my blurry eyes. My relentless battle with my thoughts and judgment continued, and I suddenly felt outnumbered.

I sensed I had seen it all before and realized in a way, I had.

When the batter with a crew cut stepped up to the plate, I knew exactly what was going to happen. He suddenly looked familiar. The whole situation became unmistakable. I stood in amusement and amazement, and for a brief moment forgot my head hurt so much.

I leaned against the fence and had a great view of the entire play. From the successive pummeling of the basemen to the sloshing of mud on every slide and collision. I could literally smell the fear in the third baseman as the runner came barreling in. Our dugout blasted with combativeness, while their dugout sounded downright militant.

As he headed for home, the ball rocketed into the catcher while the runner started his slide as far away as I'd ever seen. It was like slow motion, only faster. I could have made the call for the ump above the noise and confusion. Safe! It was the strangest déjà vu I ever experienced. Both teams erupted with equal levels of excitement but for very different reasons.

I guess he was telling the truth. Every last bit of it. I shook my head in utter astonishment. How in the world had I just witnessed the story I'd heard so many times before? My hand was still dirty from grasping the ball for goodness sake.

It was without a doubt the oddest home run I ever saw. But, man was I ecstatic. I was thrilled beyond belief in so many ways. I'd not only heard the story but had now lived it. It was real. It leapt out of my imagination, which was exhilarating yet out-and-out frightening.

Our dugout cleared and theirs did, too. The imminent clash subsided thanks to the boisterous, no nonsense ump. I guessed correctly it was Mr. Kohl.

We celebrated on the field, and I was purposely the last one to give the home run hitter a high five. As everyone continued to celebrate around us, I felt I must talk with that man.

He was my grandpa after all.

"Nice hit!" I told him. We exchanged another high five.

"Thanks, John," as he gave me a familiar nod and a wink. I guessed it wasn't the coffee that gave him twitches.

Somehow he knew my name. Of course he would. But did he really know who I was? I realized I didn't know him either, especially not the way he was then. He was about my age and had this astonishing resemblance to the man I knew, only much younger and fitter. This was truly freakish. My mind played catch-up, slackened by the clash between the thoughts in my head and the reality before my eyes.

How did he even recognize me? How did everyone else recognize me for that matter? I must have somehow, someway taken on the life of a baseball teammate.

I considered scratching my eyes and closing my head but settled on the reverse. It was the most bizarre dream I ever had. I couldn't decide whether to laugh, cry, or yell at the top of my lungs. None would have been good for my aching head. I felt caught between what did happen and what was going to happen.

"I sure showed those Hartland folks a thing or two about baseball, didn't I?" he chuckled.

His laughter was contagious. Almost as much as the pneumonia we were contracting if we stayed outside much longer.

"I'm freezing." He chattered his teeth. "Wanna come over to my place and have some dinner? All this excitement is making me hungry."

"Ah... sure. That'd be awesome," I responded. Dinner with my grandpa and his family. Really? Throw in the fact that he actually had teeth to chatter. This was getting weirder by the minute.

He jerked toward me and squinted his eyes.

"Have you flipped your wig? What do you mean by awesome?"

"Huh? It means great or amazing," I replied with a matching look of confusion. I swore I just said that word to him only a few hours earlier. Must have forgotten. Or then again, maybe it hadn't happened yet.

We packed up our stuff in the dugout. I could pick out my old, reliable baseball bag from anywhere. It was sitting in the corner, right where I left it. The same bag I had used since middle school, and the one my grandpa gave me and said it was a town relic. At least I had something I could call my own.

"Doing ok, John? Do I need to take you anywhere?" asked Coach.

"Nah, I'm fine. A bit of a headache and my eyesight's blurry, but I'll be back to normal in no time."

"Ok, you let me know if I can help. Have your mom or dad call me if there's any concern."

"Ah yeah. Thanks, Coach."

I had no idea who he was talking about or even where I lived. Did he say mom... or dad? Anxiety was about to devour me if I wasn't careful. I took a deep, extended breath. I figured I was the first person in the history of the world to travel like this. But if that was the case, then who do I ask for help? Man, my head hurt.

I have a distinct memory of my emotions at that moment, drifting from sadness to curiosity to sheer panic. But I knew for certain, this was sure going to be interesting. Very interesting.

I looked at my grandpa and tried not to let my concern show. Maybe he could tell me where I lived. Better yet, he could tell me where and when the heck it was. I knew he was no longer able to attend my games, so why was he here? Why was he playing? And what age-defying weight loss plan did he suddenly start using? I felt as unsteady as I'd ever felt.

My parents would be worried when they found out what happened. The painful injury, the traversal of existence, the unrelenting confusion. My sense of loneliness was in no way calmed by the people and places and things around me. Familiarity became a deserted friend.

I knew my grandpa well enough to know he would most certainly lead. And for the first time in my life, I would wholeheartedly follow.

Chapter 4

"You don't look so good, pal. You sure you're ok?" my grandpa inquired.

My grandpa. Such an endearing name with a hint of possessiveness to it. I considered using a different name for him since we were somehow the same age. It suddenly became unorthodox to call him Grandpa, and he would have smacked me if I did.

"Yeah, feeling fine. Just a headache. Thanks, Bill."

I tested my luck. He didn't flinch, and I guessed he shouldn't. But I'd never called him by his first name before. Why would I? It was awkward, but I didn't really have a choice.

The rain stopped coming down and the fog drifted back to the sky, so I surveyed my new surroundings. Unfortunately, everything around me appeared fuzzy and imprecise as if I wore goggles in a sauna.

Luckily, I noticed a few things. The river beyond the ball field sustained a noticeably swift current, but that was mostly from hearing the rushing sounds of the impatient water.

Above the river and beyond the rocky ledge, I caught a glimpse of the old high school.

The ball field looked exactly the same. Home to the rockiest, most uneven dirt that was there since the world began. Coach always said, 'If you can field a ground ball here, you can get one anywhere.' He was probably right.

The grass was a typical springtime mix with hues of green and brown scattered throughout. A palette of colors I'd recognize anywhere. At least it was all grass. The groundskeepers always avoided bare spots in the outfield, a sure fire way for someone to get hurt. The last thing I wanted to happen at a baseball game.

I looked back and couldn't help but notice the familiar dugouts. Same wooden structures I was accustomed to, although recently painted a clean white with navy blue stripes.

The chain-link outfield fence was starkly different. It was half the height, and there wasn't a large dent in right-center where Caleb crashed into it making his miraculous catch. Then I realized my past suddenly transformed into the future.

This was getting even more bizarre.

As we continued to walk, the questions that swirled in my head did nothing to ease my splitting headache. Most of them had nothing to do with where. The bigger questions were more a matter of when.

For starters, I guessed it was 1941. Since everything else turned out to be accurate from that game, I was pretty certain he got the year right, too. But how could that be? Last thing I remembered it was 2004, and I was 18 years old. I couldn't just snap my fingers and suddenly change the year.

He also looked about 18 to me. Looked a lot like Caleb, actually. Same muscular build. Same athletic demeanor that reeked of confidence. Caleb had this swagger that was great on the ball field but would otherwise be annoying if I didn't know him well. For my grandpa, it was a swagger he apparently lost a long time ago.

"You loved my homer at the end there, didn't ya?" He pointed his finger at me. "Man, that was tops."

"Yeah, that was really cool. Can't believe it actually happened. Did ya think you'd make it all the way home?" I walked alongside him on the sidewalk.

"Nah, not really. Honestly, I figured I'd be out at first." He darted me a perplexed look. "Whaddya mean by cool? Never heard a temperature to describe an event."

Here I thought we had a challenging language barrier before.

"Oh, I was just saying how cold it is out here... Yeah, you shoulda been out. Good thing Hartland stinks 'cause that was at least a three-base error."

"Watch it or I'll give ya a knuckle sandwich!" He extended his fist toward my face. "It was clearly a home run. No fooling. I'll letcha know when the paper calls for my interview."

He shoved me, throwing me off balance. The heavy bag I carried over my shoulder didn't help as I almost landed in a puddle next to the sidewalk. I tiptoed around it. A funny maneuver looking back on it as my shoes, my uniform, everything about me was already soaked with rain and doused in mud.

I studied him closely. While the mix of humor and subtle gruffness made him a dead giveaway, he had clearly become a teenager in both age and disposition. He owned such a young, smooth face, I wouldn't have recognized him without his crew cut. I laughed when I noticed his smaller, thinner nose.

Most everything about him threw me for a loop. The only logical explanation was he was a boy possessed by my grandfather. Some type of paranormal going-on that I'd read about in tomorrow's newspaper. I wondered if I'd lost any trace of sanity I had left.

"All I know is we'll reminisce about that game over and over again." My arm rolled in front of my chest. "Every excruciating detail."

His head angled down and his forehead creased. "What are you talkin' about?"

"Nothin'. Nothin' at all."

He didn't get it, but why should he? I wasn't about to spell it out for him, as explaining the future was a tough business to be in. How could I describe an inside joke when only I was on the inside? I felt caught between two worlds in more ways than one.

As we turned the corner onto Main Street, the distinctive oak trees came into view. Their massive trunks shot out of gaps in the sidewalk like missiles out of underground silos, and their hearty branches protected everything within their span. They're what makes it Waterville. Distinctions in both character and affinity. I paused to gaze at those towering trees.

When we passed the hardware store, I recognized the tree I ran into when I was six. My mom ran a quick errand while I rode my miniature bike on the sidewalk. She told me repeatedly to slow down, but I was out to prove how old I really was. Being all boy and fatherless made me do stupid things apparently.

But I couldn't figure out how to apply the dumb brakes. Ran right smack into the godforsaken tree. I flipped over my handlebars and socked the ground on my aching back and left arm. Didn't cry, though. Kept right on riding till my mom came out and screamed when she saw blood on my arm. 'Oh yeah, that,' I said.

I looked at Bill and could tell he was pondering deeply about something. I guess I'm more like him than I thought.

"Yeah, I won't forget that game for a while," he mumbled then suddenly perked up. "I loved their reactions: surprise from the first baseman, annoyance from second, and pure terror from third. Sure was sweet." His hand motions told even more of the story than his words.

Such an interesting coincidence. Sounded like my progression of emotions after getting slapped by that darn ball: surprise, annoyance, and fear. I was beginning to wonder what came next.

I lifted my cap, scratched my head, then put it back on. How I ended up with the same cap as him, I'll never know. Off white with blue lettering. It was even well worn and raggedy like it had taken part in too many games to count.

We continued walking down Main as the sun disappeared. A marked coolness in the air with the trees producing long, intimidating shadows. Good thing I knew them well.

The few cars on the road all flirted with me. Their provocative front grills, the huge white walls and chrome hubcaps where I admired my reflection, and the seductive, sloped trunks in the back. Headlights protruded around grills like big, beady eyes looking expectantly to wherever they traveled. And there they were, right before me in all their splendor. I wiped the drool from my mouth and wondered if there was a car heaven.

"It's about time ol' Turkey comes out of hibernation, dontcha think?" Bill pondered.

"Who or what in the blazes is ol' Turkey?" I had no clue who he was talking about.

"John, John. That ball really did whack ya." He glanced at me with a mix of concern and confusion. "We just talked about him last week during batting practice. Wow, you really don't remember, do you?"

If only he knew. Last week to him and last week to me were two very different times. We continued walking together, but only our steps were synchronized.

"Nope… But I'm sure you'll tell me about him. Why was he sleeping again?"

"Had stomach issues when he was a youngin'. Hit him hard every fall, so he stayed in bed all winter. My dad just met some fancy-dressed guy from New York doin' a story on him. Called him the human hibernator."

"That's crazy! Another eccentric from Waterville. Yeah, that ball really did set me back a few leagues." Waterville always did have a reputation to uphold, which was not necessarily a compliment.

"You better believe there's a bunch of crazies in this town. By the way, you'd better snap out of it by tomorrow 'cause we have a math test."

How could I forget about school? Crap. So many things to take in, so many things to unravel. I decided to worry about that later.

As we turned onto Fifth, I realized where we were going. I completely forgot my grandpa grew up three doors down from where I lived. The two-story brick house on the corner with the large front porch. Recognized it from a mile away.

I also peeked down at my house, at least my house from 2004. At first glance, it looked the same except some out-of-place shrubs by the front steps. All the houses on the block had barely changed across the span of decades. The narrow road with gradual hills leading to modest, tightly-packed homes.

"Should I, uh, tell my parents where I am?" I asked.

"Nah, no worries. They'll know you're with me. They always assume that."

How cool was that? We were buddies. While I missed my mom and sister back home – Caleb, too – I considered how this might actually turn out to be fun. Relatively speaking, of course. At least my grandpa would live a story or two rather than regurgitate them.

We walked into Bill's house. The place was small yet sparse, and the furniture was colorful but flat. The living room chairs looked like they were carved from stone, and unfortunately, were as hard as they looked. The Flintstones would have felt more at home than I did. At least they were a deep crimson that livened up the place.

There were other oddities that tossed me a curve ball. The television was replaced by a large contraption with dials I assumed was a radio, and instead of a refrigerator they had an ice box. So while in some ways this might be fun, it would have to be done without my Mountain Dew and *Friends*.

* * *

"Dinner sure was… uh, good. Thanks!" I told his mom. I really needed to teach myself how to talk back then. Awesome? Cool? Forget it.

I had forgotten how large of a family my grandpa came from. He had five sisters and a younger brother, all walking, talking replicas of each other. His sister, Eleanor, told a story, and I swore it was Bill in a dress and a wig. Creepy. Good thing the story was hilarious so I could disguise my laughter. Neither would have appreciated my observation.

His mom and dad were fairly quiet. With all the talking from their seven kids, I could see why. I recognized most of them from pictures. Honestly, I had only met his younger brother, Donny, but even that was a long time ago. The girls had all died young, so I never got to meet any of them. At least, until that day.

And that first day was such a blur. It didn't occur to me until later that I had just met my great-grandparents, aunts, and uncles. Turns out, they were all great. The unmistakable family resemblance, the odd sense of humor that forced me to laugh.

I would get my chance later to again enjoy their company.

"I should probably head home. Thanks again for the meal," I said as I took my plate and disappeared into the kitchen. Bill followed me in.

"I'll walk you home, John."

Thank goodness. I couldn't tell him I had no idea where I lived. Although, I should ask all the asinine questions early. The ball to the head excuse only lasts so long.

"That'd be great," I confided.

I hoisted my baseball bag over my shoulder, and we headed out the front door. Their spacious front porch was one big conversation waiting to happen. I couldn't wait to test it out, but I was exhausted.

Bill walked ahead of me. It felt good to be near him, as if he suddenly became my tour guide to a foreign land. While dinner provided a nice respite, my heart exploded as we walked down the sidewalk. My eyes drifted from houses to cars to trees, and there were so many changes from the reality I knew. The sidewalk was more uneven and the trees a lot younger. I spotted a few I could leap over in a single bound, the same ones I normally had to strain to see their tops. But choppy walkways and tree growth were the least of my worries.

Turned out, my house was where I lived. That is, I was about to enter the same house I lived in back home with my mom and Sarah. Although the house appeared the same, the time was apparently over sixty years in the past. Exact same brick in every shade of brown imaginable, a tiered walkway leading to a porch with an overhang, brown rutted grass, and the stupid detached garage out back.

The house became another element in this wacky time warp that I assumed meant something.

I was conflicted. While so much had changed, so much had also stayed the same. The slowness of change that drove me nuts as a kid, I suddenly found reassuring.

"See ya at school tomorrow, Bill."

"Let's walk together. You can tell me everything I need to know in math. Easier than studying." He patted me on my back.

I laughed. Sounded exactly like something I'd say. "Yeah, that'd be great. Have a good night, buddy."

He shook his head then snapped it as he spoke, "There you go again… buddy…"

Bill strutted down the sidewalk. I smiled, just to myself.

As I was about to enter my house, my mind swept ahead by a flood of anxiety. Like Christmas morning with gifts galore under the tree, except the people around me were strangers. The differences, the similarities, all in one convoluted mess.

I inhaled as much fresh air as my lungs could hold, then swung open the door. "Hey Mom," I yelled. I was so enthralled to meet my family, I was surprised I didn't disintegrate the door with any foot, hand, or sledgehammer within reach.

"Don't forget about me, Son. How was your game?" came a deep, throaty voice from the living room.

I'll never forget the way my heart skipped a beat, a beat I didn't know I could live without. Even in my muddled state, I savored the sweetness of the words. Surprised me how quickly the memory rushed back. But it was distinct and pointed like the sharp tip of a needle.

He shot me an expectant smile. He wore khaki pants and a dark blue collared shirt tucked in tightly around the waist. As I entered the house, I distinctly smelled the pipe that dangled from his mouth. He positioned the newspaper on top of the end table, then rose up from his chair and walked toward me. I sensed the hurriedness in his step.

I dropped my baseball bag in the foyer, where I normally put it actually. I stuck out my hand to greet him and beamed with only half the smile I wanted to give. I took off my wet cap to avert my gaze and cover the sudden and unexpected dampness of my eyes.

I wiped them, a bit embarrassed. But I couldn't have been happier. For the first time in as long as I could remember, a man had just called me Son.

Chapter 5

"It was an awesome game, Dad. Bill won it with a home run!" I attempted to contain my excitement, but I sounded more like a pint-sized kid who just scored a victory in a Little League game.

I followed him back to the living room, and he sat in the big, red chair next to the end table. He pushed the paper to the side, grabbed his coffee mug, and took a swig. Who exactly was this man? And how was I sitting with him in a room that reeked of familiarity yet appeared so dated and different?

The walls were painted a light green, and the floor was covered with a dull, colorless carpet. As I expected, the fireplace was in the same spot, right across from the large, open walkway. Funny thing was I remembered seeing bits of that green paint right by the edge of the mantel when I repainted the room with Sarah two years earlier.

"Great to hear, Son. How'd you do?" He could call me that as many times as he wanted.

I took a seat in the brown suede chair opposite the table. It was remarkably comfortable but felt like it was missing something. Then I realized it was not a La-Z-Boy recliner. It didn't move.

The old-time radio sat on the table between us, which I could see out of the corner of my eye. However, my gaze did not divert from watching the man who was apparently my father. In my new life, that is.

"Pretty good. Had two hits and scored a run in the first. But I also got smacked by a hard liner." I quickly realized I was confusing games. I never actually went to bat in the game he was referring to.

The pain continued, but the entire incident was forgotten until I brought it up. I reluctantly pointed to the bump on my temple and gave it a good rub. It felt soft and tender like a half-filled water balloon.

"Yeah, looks like a rough one." He stretched out his neck to get a good view. "You'll be feeling that for a while. Why don't you get out of your wet clothes and head to bed. I know you have a big day at school tomorrow."

"You're right, probably should. Have a good night, Dad."

He took the name in stride. I liked that.

I sat up from the chair, turned around, and noticed how wet it had become from me sitting on it. I had completely forgotten how soaked my uniform was.

I headed toward the wide, oak staircase, already knowing where the rooms were upstairs. A few steps up, I turned to my left and glanced at my dad sitting in the living room. With his pipe back in his mouth, he ruffled the newspaper, bending it in half to read the next page. From my vantage point, his gray hair peeked just above it.

I found my room at the end of the hallway on the right. As I walked across the cold oak flooring, I noticed a few baseball trophies on the dresser. I instinctively grabbed the larger one on the right, a decorative red framework resting on a white marble base with a golden slugger in mid-swing at its crest. Looked like they won the state championship the year prior. Come to think of it, I did recall my grandpa mentioning that a while back. They pulled out the championship with a five-run rally in the sixth. I didn't believe him, but I was beginning to second-guess myself.

I stripped off my damp clothes and laid them on the chair by the dresser. My muscles felt taut and achy like my day consisted of a long, continuous sprint. I rubbed my smooth chest then lined the grooves of my rib cage between my fingers. As a teenager, I normally slept the way God made me (as my grandpa called it), but I was just feeling awfully cold that night. My whole body shook as the room suddenly felt drafty. The uncovered oak flooring didn't help, as I missed the carpeting I normally had in my room.

It was awkward putting on someone else's clothes, but the frigid, rain-soaked contest left me no choice. I found some plain, white pajamas in the top drawer of the dresser and slid them on. I had not worn pajamas since I was a little kid, but the soft flannel against my clammy, damp skin felt like I was the first to discover something new for all of mankind.

I crawled into bed, but excitement and sleep were a horrible mix. I stared at the ceiling wondering what my life would be like and asking myself questions I never thought I'd ask. Was this permanent? Certainly, my mom and Sarah were worried about me. Or maybe they didn't even know I was gone. I was surprised I even cared what they thought. But I did. How would I ever get back to my other life? Maybe I died and this was an unknown arrangement of heaven? For all I knew, it was hell.

The sensation resembled the first night of summer camp. Being away from home and looking forward to what the week may hold were enough to prevent even the heartiest from sleeping. Making new friends, playing new games, and swimming till the sun went down. What could be any better?

But in the back of my mind lingered apprehension. Maybe it was the change of so many things at once. The town, the school, my baseball team, my family and friends, the decade for Christ's sake. What if I got homesick? What if I had just fallen into oblivion and no one noticed? What if I was stuck here forever?

There was such a thin line between the best times and worst times of my life, and I was never quite sure when or where that line got crossed.

* * *

Someone came in to wake me, but unfortunately, I only caught a glimpse of her as she walked out the door. The sun had not risen yet, so the brilliance of the overhead light overwhelmed my senses. I heard a muffled clanging down the hall and assumed it was Sarah. She always got up before I did so she could spend an hour in the bathroom.

Back in those days, I bargained for extra sleep whenever I got the chance. I'd lie prostrate across the far corners of the bed, mumble into my pillow, and basically do a pathetic job of convincing myself to wake up. Somehow, I always lost the argument.

I sat up in bed, then caught a heavy dose of truth when I brushed back my hair and felt the bump on my head. What happened yesterday? My shaken memory was of little help. I did recall playing baseball. That I'd never forget. For the good and the bad of it, beyond that was one big, empty void.

Once I realized Sarah was not in the bathroom, I hurried there to take a shower. The hot water felt good against my lean, muscular body as I rubbed the clamminess off my waterlogged skin. I'm not normally one to brag, but I loved the way I looked during baseball season. I must have been in there for ten minutes trying to recollect so much of what happened. I stepped out of the shower, glanced over at the fogged vanity, and suddenly realized where I was.

Or should I say when I was.

I slipped on what I guessed were school clothes then headed downstairs for breakfast. My dad was already eating at the table, and the woman who came in to wake me was cooking eggs and bacon. She wore a green dress with a multicolored floral pattern that I could only describe as motherly. That alone told me what I needed to know.

"Hey Mom and Dad. Mornin'," I greeted as cheerily as I could muster. Funny how I always rub my eyes when I say something laced with uncertainty.

I waited patiently for Sarah to call me Eeyore, but then I realized there was no Sarah. I would have told them about being compared to a moody, depressed donkey, but I also realized these people would have no idea what I was talking about.

Speaking of which, how was I supposed to talk to these two? I felt like an actor thrown into a play where everyone else knew the script. I tried hard not to freak out, but it was an explosive inside me ticking away.

"Good Morning, John! Your eggs are almost ready," my mom said with an annoying cheeriness.

"Mornin', Son. Did you sleep well or did that bump on your head get the best of you?" my dad asked. At least one of us remembered the conversation from the night before.

"I slept pretty well, actually. Does it look bad?"

"You barely notice, John," he answered while taking a bite of food. I barely knew the guy, but I could tell he was lying through his teeth.

"Here's your eggs, Son." She slid my plate on the table then reached down and dabbed my forehead. "Your father told me what happened. That should heal just fine, but I'd take it easy for a couple of days."

It was charming to have a woman in my life to bring a voice of caution, sense, and downright dullness. It was baseball season. There was no plausible way I'd be slowing down anytime soon.

I ate my eggs in three bites; the bacon in one.

"Gotta run. Meeting Bill to walk to school. See ya!"

I dashed out the front door faster than they could say goodbye and caught Bill walking down the sidewalk. I sported a huge grin and waved, but quickly realized I was acting like a moronic middle schooler. I dampened my enthusiasm.

"Hey Bill! Doing well?"

"Sure thing. Slept like a baby. How 'bout you? How's that second head you're growing coming along?"

"Not too bad but haven't named it yet. Still hurts like a bear but feelin' better."

"Don't mean to rag ya. Let me know when my humor runs out of gas."

I looked at him hoping I understood what the heck he just said.

We turned the corner heading toward the high school. It was a brisk morning, but the wool sweater I found in the closet kept me warmer than ever. I briefly considered my calling as a sheep farmer. Maybe in my third life.

"So... do you like Anna?" He caught me by surprise.

"Uh, yeah... sure. Why do you ask?" I tried to dodge the question, hoping my blank stare didn't give it away that I had never met her before in my life.

"Just thinkin' about asking her out. Whaddya think there, Ace?"

He shot me an expectant look with raised eyebrows, so I knew the answer he was hoping for. "Sure, why not?"

I kicked a rock by the edge of the sidewalk and landed it smack dab in the middle of the puddle I aimed at. More and more kids surrounded us as we approached school grounds. Many walked in groups, a few rode cruiser bikes with wide tires and long handlebars resembling bent golf clubs.

"Well, she's a dish and all, but I'm not sure she likes me." He tilted his head and looked at me. "I mean, she acts funny. Why just the other day, she slid on over to the other side of the hallway like she thought I had the plague. I don't get it."

Clearly this man had never been in love. Such a strange thought – a girl playing hard to get with my grandpa.

"Why don't you ask her out, Bill? She'd like that. Positive."

We walked down Francis and crossed the bridge over the Rock River. The current had subsided from the deluge I recollected from the night before. We headed toward the parking lot when I faintly recognized someone walking toward us. As he grabbed something out of his school bag, I trusted this town was as safe as I remembered.

"Hey Eddy. What's up?" asked Bill.

"Doing great. Fun game last night, huh boys?" Eddy said. "Man that was dynamite. I've never seen anything like that ending before. Hey, I thought you should have this."

Bill and I both glanced down at his hand and instantly recognized it. It was smothered in dirt and still noticeably damp from the night before. Bill snatched the ball out of Eddy's hand and tossed it straight up in the air. As he caught it, he dropped his shoulder then tackled me like a linebacker. We all chuckled at his realistic yet slightly exaggerated recreation of events.

"Thanks for saving the ball for me, Eddy. That's really sharp!"

Bill hurled it in the air a few more times, then placed it in his school bag for safe keeping. He retold the entire story, knowing full well both Eddy and I had witnessed the whole darn thing the night before. His arms flailed, and his voice was loud and intense. The puddles of mud, the unavoidable collisions, the monstrous slide home, the suspense of the game-deciding call. Every last detail.

There was no doubt who he was.

But while I listened to his story for the umpteenth time, I sensed a sudden and distinct realization. I had seen that ball before. I even grasped it in my hand and admired the crusty, old dirt and barely visible seams. I even knew where it was stored for safe keeping.

"Can I see that ball, Bill?"

He rustled the books and papers in his bag and eventually found it. He pulled it out, glimpsed at it, then flipped the muddy ball over to me. As I tossed it around, my memory surged back like I cradled a crystal ball. It shocked my hand. It jolted my imagination. I swore we just sat down at our kitchen table to inspect it.

I handed it back to him, exchanging it for his unforgettable expression of thrill and triumph. His prize achievement. I'm not usually one to guess what other people think, but this time I knew.

Chapter 6

I always assumed school was the same no matter which decade I attended. The teachers talked a lot, the half-listening students sent notes around to stay awake, then I'd go home one day closer to post-school freedom. Boy was I wrong.

I felt like I had stepped into either a time warp or a coming-of-age movie about the 1940s. Every step brought me deeper into an abyss of strangeness, and it gave me the willies. All the girls sported long, flowing dresses, and we boys snazzed up in collared shirts and dress pants. My normal shorts and T-shirt would have made me the oddball in that crowd. Good thing I grabbed the right clothes.

The building was puny compared to mine. There were two floors, but I could stand in the middle and see the stairwells on both ends. I'm guessing there were only a few hundred students, not surprising for a thriving metropolis like Waterville.

Bill, Eddy, and I walked down the wide hallway. I purposely followed one step behind since I had no clue where I was going. However unassuming that little school was, I concealed the fact that it scared the living bejeebers out of me.

They kept right on flapping their lips, but I couldn't tell for the life of me what they chatted about. My mind raced ahead, much faster than my feet could walk. Bill and Eddy took a left past the cafeteria, and we headed up the open stairway. I continued trailing a step behind.

Our unobstructed walk up the stairs was much easier than I was used to. People actually walked on the right side of the stairs in an orderly fashion. It was proper, courteous, and downright weird. At my school, it was a free-for-all, both up and down. Slide down the railing or, even more daring, walk on the left side. Not here.

As we entered what must have been the senior hallway, I noticed some guys from the baseball team. I said 'hi', which put me slightly more at ease. Bill and Eddy found their lockers and started getting their books ready for the first class of the day.

Not knowing where my locker was located was the least of my worries. I had no idea what my classes were for the day let alone which rooms they were in.

"You look dazed and confused, Johnny boy. How hard that ball slug ya yesterday?" Bill pointed out, more correctly than he ever knew. He grabbed two books as I stood nearby and watched.

"Yeah, that must be it," I tried to laugh it off. "I'm not sure I even know what my classes are today. Isn't that odd?"

Bill joined me in my laughter, however, his more restrained. I suspected he thought I should be headed for the nut farm. Can't say I blame him.

"Well, come with me. You're in luck! Your first three classes are with little ol' me." He tucked his books against his chest and tilted his head to the side. His grin was cheesy.

I've never heard anyone call him little before, but I wasn't about to correct him.

He pointed me to my locker so I gathered my books and we headed to Geometry. I was in luck – I had that class two years prior. The classroom was way down at the end of the hall, so it was a good thing we were fast runners. We arrived as the bell clanged.

The small room was filled with wooden chairs that had wraparound tops connected to the seats. All in neatly defined rows. A large oak desk sat near the front with a vast black board of infinite possibilities behind it. The teacher stood nearby, wearing a dark brown suit with his arms folded like he wanted to start class five minutes earlier.

As class progressed, the teacher fascinated me. Not because he was interesting, but because of his obsessive use of chalk. He was constantly surrounded by a cloud of dust and his formerly nice clothes were covered with its remnants. I would have gotten in trouble if I had called him Pigpen, but I swear that was what he looked like.

Back when I was eight, Sarah and I had a miniature easel that we used for drawing pictures. We possessed an assortment of colored chalk, but I used a lot of red. Sarah's beautiful drawings of flowers and rabbits were no match for the scorched earth effects of my fire-breathing dragons. She never appreciated that come to think of it.

My classes were composed almost entirely of boys. I was completely oblivious to that fact until our third class of the day which Bill told me was called Reading. Eddy was in the front row taking his turn to read. Since Bill and I sat way in the back, I leaned toward Bill as quietly as I could.

"Where are the girls?" I asked.

"The dollies have their own classes, knucklehead," Bill whispered.

"What? Girls are the spice of life! They don't have germs, at least not since middle school."

"You're hilarious, Johnny." He shook his head. "They take homemaker classes where they wash clothes and make dinner. You know, the important stuff."

"John and Bill! Be quiet back there!" hollered the teacher. He also wore a dark brown suit as if it were a uniform, but at least he steered clear of the chalk.

I massaged my temple. I still didn't know how he or anybody else knew my name.

All the other kids turned to watch me, including the two girls sitting up front. Nothing like making a fool of myself on my first day at a school. That was the last thing I wanted.

"Good thing he doesn't have lasers for eyes," I joked.

"Huh?" Bill's chin snapped back into his neck, then his upper body spasmed to shake the confusion. "Anyway, do I have to tell the school nurse about you? You should go anyway just because she's cute. Actually, let me go for you... cough! cough!"

Bill had many wonderful traits. Acting was not one of them.

"Would you boys hush back there! One more outburst and you're both headed to the principal's office," the teacher bellowed. His face turned the curious shade of a radish, which scared me enough to at least consider keeping quiet.

I leaned back into my seat and grinned. My arms folded around my chest in an effort to contain myself. One hand reached up to cover my mouth and conceal my amusement, but the scolding look from the teacher told me I didn't do a very good job of it. He looked like a lion ready to pounce on his prey. A red-faced lion, that is.

"Thanks," I whispered in Bill's direction.

* * *

The last class of the day was physical education. We entered the gymnasium through a door marked "Boys Only." The instructor lined us single file, then led a militaristic march toward mats lined up on the floor. We each sat on one and performed peculiar stretches he called calisthenics. Felt more like contortionist training. He then told us to get ready for swimming and meet him in the pool area.

I followed Bill and the other guys into the locker room. The skinny, red-haired kid told a story about his dog getting his head stuck in a bucket that he couldn't shake. Poor, embarrassed dog. At least he had a place to hide his head in shame.

Rows of blue metal lockers lined the walls with a long, wooden bench down the middle. We randomly split into two groups and took both sides of the bench. There were more than enough lockers for each of us.

As the other boys started removing their clothes, I did as well. Then I realized I was missing something. We were all missing something.

"Bill, where's the swimsuits?" I asked from the side of my mouth as I rubbed my eye with my open hand. I really didn't want anyone else to hear my embarrassing predicament.

Bill stopped what he was doing and flashed me a smirk. He chuckled at my joke. Little did he know, it was in no way intended as a joke.

"We swim the way God made us, dear John!" he answered in a loud, booming voice. He stretched out his arms, looking up in a mocking gesture. His shirt was off at that point, but his pants were still on. Thank goodness. Some other boys glanced over and joined him in his laughter.

"Seriously?" I whispered, attempting to reel back the conversation.

"Why not, John? You embarrassed?" asked Henry, a tall, muscular kid with blonde hair, blue eyes, and an attitude the size of Illinois. He stood on the other side of the bench and shot me a sinister look like he was a newly inducted Gestapo agent. I despised the jackass.

"No, not at all. Just thought I'd ask." I pumped out my chest. And prepared for the inevitable.

The pool door swung open, and a cool breeze rushed in.

"Hurry up in there!" The instructor was agitated by our slowness.

We all continued undressing as fast as we could then lined up near the pool edge. It was a small pool surrounded by light blue tiles with wooden boards around the outer walls. A diving board extended over the deep end with four-row bleachers along the side wall. Thank God they were empty.

Everything was normal enough, except we were all completely and utterly naked. Head to toe. The way God made us.

When my only saving grace was cupped hands in a strategic location, I knew embarrassment had settled in. I tried acting like the other guys who had evidently done this many times before. But I was positive I stood out like a big, white polar bear on a bright, sunny beach. A naked polar bear, that is.

Any color my skin may have turned, whether it was from humiliation or shivering from the exposed chill, was certainly clear for all to see. The noticeable circulation of cold, damp air only served as a reminder of how unprotected I was.

Let me translate: my butt was cold.

I was certainly not about to look around to see where the breeze was coming from. I saw enough already. And that included seeing more of my grandpa than I ever hoped for or intended. A disturbing nightmare no matter how I describe it.

At least gravity had not taken its toll as the cruelest force of nature.

The worst part was lining up for roll call. We arranged ourselves along the side of the pool and were required to raise a hand when our name was called. Good thing God gave me two of them.

Why roll call? Didn't we just see him in the gym? What was I going to do, run away? Actually, I wish I had thought of that. But I'd only streak if someone paid me money. A lot of money.

I was relieved when roll call finally finished so we could hop into the warm water. The suspense was killing me.

We all plunged in then performed a peculiar kicking warm-up while holding on to the edge. I snickered at its simplicity. The rest of the time, we had free rein to swim around the pool.

"C'mon out and join us, John!" yelled Bill from the edge of the diving board. He reminded me of a chicken lining up for slaughter.

"Ah, no thanks. Not today," I replied from the protective confines of the water below.

Everyone else was brave enough to dive off the diving board, but I had no intention of getting out of the water unless I had to. To my relief, class finally finished, commencing another parade of all boy nakedness. The showers were the last hurrah before my clothes became my new best friend.

The last week of school I actually dove off the diving board. I did one of those 'hey, look, there's a girl' tricks to distract everyone from watching. It didn't work, but I felt better to at least make an effort.

I thought I had heard every story from every nook and cranny of my grandpa's past. Everything from his grand stories about baseball to the pellet stuck in his temple after his brother shot him with a BB gun. He neglected to mention swimming class. I think I figured out why.

All in all, my first day at school felt like it lasted forever. After an easy math class and one frightening swim class later, it was time to head home. Although I went through some eye-opening things that day, my thoughts always snapped back to dwelling on one thing. And it had nothing to do with swimming.

While I obviously wondered why I was there, I decided there was no rush to figure that one out. I truly believed there was a reason for everything. I must have been put there for something, and I figured in due time I would be told why.

But there was definitely a more pressing issue that haunted me. A feeling that I was exposed to something different, something out of this world.

There was a question I needed to ask and a quick investigation I needed to perform. I had no clue what the answer was, but I was bound and determined to find out.

I needed to find the one thing that captured my imagination ever since I saw it... again.

And I hoped the ball was right where I left it.

Chapter 7

When the final bell rang, I dashed home as fast as my legs could take me. I whizzed down Main Street, counting the immense oaks I passed like seconds on a stopwatch.

Many doors were propped open as the warm afternoon sun shone brightly across town. I stuffed my wool sweater in my backpack to enjoy the newfound pleasant weather. My untucked shirt flapped behind me in the backdraft.

It was a popular day to be out walking. Only a few cars were on the road, and a handful more parked by the curb. I loved the idea of using my legs to take me places. Not a typical sight in my normally car-obsessed world.

But while a stroll around town seemed jolly, I was beelining for home as fast as I could. The only problem was everyone around me was going slower than a horse-drawn carriage. While I hoped for a conveyer belt, I ended up with an obstacle course.

An older lady came out of Montgomery Ward and stepped out on the sidewalk directly in front of me. She wore an eye-catching pink scarf covering her bushy grey hair and a large winter coat too heavy for the conditions. She should have checked the weather on her smartphone. If only she knew.

I just about knocked the poor lady over. My quick spin did the trick as I carefully scooted around her. I glanced back at her, managed a quick smile, then caught a glimpse of her nasty, burning scowl. For the most part, everyone after that stayed out of my way.

I leapt up the front steps of my house and dashed in the front door. The screen slammed behind me. I glanced down to the linoleum floor. My baseball bag was gone.

"Afternoon, John! You're home early. Nice day at school?" My mom greeted me from the kitchen.

"Where's my bag?" I shouted back.

I heard her put something down then walk slowly toward the foyer. I was startled by the olive green apron she wore. While it was no doubt an attractive color, I had just never seen anyone wear an apron before.

"Now John, please don't be so rude. I noticed how everything was wet this morning, so I cleaned it out for you. That must have been some muddy game! The bag's in the garage and everything I found in it is upstairs in your room. By the way, what's the..."

Before she could finish, I darted up the stairs, landing hard on each expectant step. I flew into my room and accidentally struck my dresser. Luckily, the trophies stayed intact.

My bat and glove rested comfortably on the middle of the bed. The sheets and blanket were perfectly tucked around the edges of the bed, while the glove was wrapped around the wooden bat with the pocket facing upward to dry it out.

Sitting right next to them was the box under the spotlight of the midday sun. As I surveyed the scene, I was not sure what surprised me more: the fact that my bed resembled an advertisement for chewing gum, or that my mom made my bed while I was at school. I started to pay attention to details I normally didn't pay attention to, and it drove me nuts.

While the bat and glove scene added a nice touch of Americana to my nostalgic room, the one item I desired was the box. I lunged for it, landing right next to it on my bed. The bat and glove hovered in the air then bounded back, but I had a good hold on the box. It wasn't going anywhere.

My heart pounded hard in my chest with my breathing labored. It surprised me as a run like that was usually effortless during baseball season.

I elevated the mysterious box and rotated it from side to side. It was clearly the same box as the one my grandpa gave me, yet it appeared so much newer. It smelled of fresh pine with a new coat of lacquer. I ran my hands along the rounded cover to experience the smooth finish that would make any woodworker proud. The golden hinges in back showed no signs of rust, and the lock looked like it had just been bought at a hardware store.

I focused on my one remaining obstacle. That darn lock. I jiggled it, hoping it would somehow open. But to no avail.

"Ah!" I moaned.

I heard my mom head to the bottom of the stairs to investigate my ruckus. "Everything all right up there, John?"

"Fine."

I realized there was a key. A key my grandpa grasped tightly in his hand then handed to me to open the box. I retraced the steps in my mind. As I sat at the kitchen table attempting to do my math homework, he plopped the box right next to my book. We carefully opened it and inspected the items. They seemed so small and insignificant to me then. Why did I suddenly care?

I remembered where it was. It hit me like a blasted liner taking square aim on its intended target. After my mom and sister came home, I was positive I had placed the key in my baseball bag. I ran to the top of the stairs.

"Mom! Where'd you put my bag?" I yelled.

She again came out of the kitchen and peeked around the corner looking toward the big staircase. Her apron swung around the doorway, for an instant making her look larger than she actually was.

"John, what are you doing up there? I can help you later if you'd like, but I really have to get dinner going. We're having..."

"Mom, I don't need your help, I just need to know where my damn bag is. I need something out of it."

I heard her sigh as she took off her apron and walked slowly to the bottom of the stairs. She put her hand on her hip and slowly glared up at me.

"What has gotten into you, John? You seem so different today. One day you're going to school and playing baseball and the next you're yelling at me from upstairs. Now I really don't appreciate your tone nor your language. Your father or I can help you later, but I'm really busy right now."

I glanced down at my feet, emitted a deep sigh, then shut my eyes. I envisioned my grandpa sliding into home on a sloppy field, the catcher eagerly anticipating the arrival of the rain-soaked baseball. The real reason I cared. The thought coerced a grin and persuaded me to reopen my eyes. I could see. She was right.

"I'm sorry, Mom. It's just... a lot has happened in the last day." More than she would ever know or understand. "I just have this box I received from... a friend of mine. I need the key to open it, and I left it in my baseball bag."

"After I cleaned out the bag, I left it in the garage. I was wondering what that box was. You'll have to show me sometime."

In my hurriedness, I heard the location but completely missed her other comments. My head nodded in acknowledgement before I made a few large leaps down the stairs. I gave my mom a hug as I passed, then headed quickly to the garage.

It was a single car garage that we normally kept stocked with junk. In comparison, this felt downright homelike. A few tools hung on the wall near a small workbench, all arranged by size and type. Just past the tools, the bag rested comfortably against the wall hanging from a large nail. I yanked it down, placed it on the workbench, then tried to remember where I had stored that stupid key. The inside pocket was a logical place, so I jerked the zipper to open it.

"Yes!"

The polished, shiny appearance was remarkable, and the elaborateness of it was just as I recalled. It was the kind of key that would unbolt an elaborate entryway to a secluded estate. I knew one day I would decipher what it spelled out, what it meant. But the complexity of it warranted multiple answers.

I ran back in the house and up the stairs to my room.

The key fit easily so I quickly removed the lock and placed it next to me on the bed. I took out each item one by one and carefully spread them out across the blanket. Each was just as I remembered them to be.

Except the one I was looking for. The one I really wanted. I lifted up the box and looked around, thinking I had missed it. Or it rolled away.

But it was not there. Even most of the scraps of mud were gone.

I knew I had seen it at the table, and I was positive we returned it. My grandpa handed it to me when my mom came home, and I placed the muddy ball in the box. I knew I did.

I lay back on the bed and stared up at the ceiling. My hands raised and slipped behind my head. The items from the box slid against me like a dog hoping to be petted.

That ball was supposed to be there. It was supposed to always be there. My typical arsenal of reasoning didn't help, nor did my usual over-thinking. Disappointment sank in like a large rain cloud, and the irony was not lost on me. A deep exhalation forced me to close my eyes. I quickly opened them, disappointed to see I was still there. And the ball was not.

It's hard for me to describe how frustrated I was at that point. I slowly put the other items back in, wondering what they could possibly mean to me. Did I miss their significance from other stories he had told me?

I checked again, making certain I had grabbed all the remaining objects. Even though the box still contained a number of items, it somehow held a sense of emptiness to it. The lid closed without a sound and fit perfectly onto the top of the box. I debated if I needed to or not but ultimately decided to secure it with the lock.

The box fit nicely on top of the dresser next to the trophies. I stored it away, not fully appreciating its significance but hoping that revelation would come sooner rather than later. Whatever lesson it was trying to teach me then, I couldn't say I liked it very much.

I stared out the window, concerning myself more with the present. I became selfish, wishing there was something I could count on, something I knew would always be there for me. The box had played that role for a short time, but that was suddenly up for debate.

I briefly considered the role could be filled by a person, but I knew that wasn't the case. My past served as my protective shield, the armory required for the fights I have fought. But it also served as a barrier, a means of keeping enemies at bay, whoever they may be. Some were obvious, like my father back home. He left as soon as responsibility looked him in the eye and challenged him to a duel. He lost. Wimp. Others I didn't know. Too many rigid memories with too many unfilled gaps.

I focused on a big maple tree in the front yard beginning to show signs of life again. A few colorful buds sat precariously on its extended branches. I could almost hear the tree breathing, wanting to come alive and speak. It knew so much, but it just stood there. Never uttering a single word.

Chapter 8

"John! Are ya comin'?"

The faint voice stirred me awake, even though I had no idea who or what it came from. I kicked my sheets around forcing them to slide down the bed. The cold draft reminded me of their worth, so I unconsciously pulled the sheets back up. I tried to ignore the chatter I thought had come from inside my half-asleep, messed up head.

As my eyes began to slowly shut under their heavy weight, a loud bang startled my whole body into a short, uncontrolled spasm. I rubbed my eyes, then placed my hands behind me to prop myself up. A cramp in my right leg came out of nowhere so I grabbed it tightly, forcing me to fall backward on my pillow.

My morning folly suddenly made me aware of my innate sense that I was being watched.

I scratched my head in a back and forth motion, ruffling my already tousled hair. Speaking of which, I realized at school I should consider getting a haircut. Pronto. Coach Finch always made sure we didn't look like girls out on the ball field, but compared to the other crew cuts and Cary Grant wannabes, mine looked downright disastrous.

I didn't think I moved all night as I felt like a wooden plank on a ship lost at sea. If it was any consolation, at least the bump on my head subsided ever so slightly. It was still easy to find, however, so I reached up and gave it a good rub.

I perceived the sounds were coming from outside. I sat up and forced my stiff body to trudge toward the window, easing the curtains open a sliver. But the brightness of the sun made my eyes water. I squinted and glanced out my window toward the front yard.

I inspected the maple tree again but quickly discounted the idea it had decided to speak. I felt sorry for it as its branches sagged from the weight of my disappointment. So, while it did communicate, it was just not in the way I had hoped.

I followed the trunk of the tree down to the ground and realized I recognized a person standing right next to it. He held an arsenal of rocks in his hands, impatiently waiting until his friend woke up.

I opened my window. The chilliness of the air hit hard against my body and forced me to tighten every muscle in my stomach. I wrapped my arms around my bare chest, a poor attempt at protecting myself.

"Hey Bill! What's up?" I yelled.

"You still comin' for our pickup game?" He looked at his watch. "It's 8:10, and the guys said they'd be there at 8:30."

I considered this proposal for a moment. But in any scenario my mind could create, baseball won out over my morning grogginess. I'd always play baseball.

"Sure! Be right down."

I threw on my baseball pants and suddenly realized it must be Saturday. I perked up with this collision of hope and reality, because it sure didn't seem like we were heading to school. Considering my messy hair, my injured head, and the disorientation of living in a completely different life, I really needed a break from school.

I grabbed my bag and headed downstairs. The clattering of my bag against the railing alerted my dad sitting in the living room. I could faintly hear the radio and wondered what he was listening to, not that I was up on my 1940s radio shows by that point.

"Hey John, did you want some breakfast before you head out?" He stood up from his chair.

"I'd love some but gotta run. Bill's waiting for me outside." I waved a polite goodbye.

As I rushed out the door, I heard my dad yell. I turned around and peeked back in.

"You forgot your cap," he pointed out as he trotted to the doorway. How could I forgot my cap? A baseball player's not a baseball player without his cap. I grabbed it and headed out again.

"Mornin' John! Have a good night, sleepyhead?" Bill asked.

"Yup, sure did. That is, until the artillery brigade bombarded my window." I gave him a nudge on his shoulder, forcing him to take a few stutter steps.

"Hey, I used whatever firepower was needed." He held up his hands then forced a laugh. "Or whatever I found on the ground. Anyway, I stood out here for five minutes wondering if you'd gotten lost in your bed."

We walked down the tiered walkway then turned right at the sidewalk.

"Nah, I'm fine. I'm always up for baseball, even if it is so early in the morning."

"What do ya mean? It's halfway through the day."

I groaned at his response and wondered how many times I had heard that before.

We walked further and headed toward Cutler Street. I knew where we were going. There have been many stories told about the old paper mill down by the lake, but I wasn't sure if and when it actually existed. One of those town legends, I figured. Rumor had it the old barn was haunted by none other than ol' Mr. Boomer. I definitely didn't believe that for a second. Heck, maybe I'd even get to meet the man himself.

"So, what do you think about Carl, Edward, and the others heading off to that war in Europe?" he asked me in the most nonchalant tone.

My legs suddenly stopped moving. I glared at him, my eyes milky and unfocused as if something bright had flashed before my eyes. It was 1941 and the world was perilously at war. At least most of the world was. All the moisture in my throat went straight to my hands, as I couldn't even hold a thought.

I started walking again and lost my footing over a large crack in the sidewalk. The roots from a massive tree had popped through the ground and fractured the sidewalk. Completely ruined the walkway for a stretch but then suddenly became flat and unaffected. An annoyingly bumpy path albeit short in length.

"I didn't think we got involved until Pearl Harbor," I blurted. By sheer instinct, I covered my mouth. He paused to pick up a rock along the sidewalk but then continued walking. He threw it in the air and caught it a few times with his hand against his chest.

"I have no idea what you're talking about, John. There ain't no harbor of pearls or whatever you call it. You need more sleep, kid. All I know is Carl and his brother are headin' over the ocean, and nobody knows if and when they're coming back."

We kept marching toward Boomer's mill which Bill said was a few blocks away. At least that morning, I was unquestionably awake and thinking clearly. The crispness in the air was enough to wake up a pile of dry bones at the graveyard.

"So, how do you feel about it?" I asked him, steering the conversation back to the original question. Honestly, I didn't know what to answer. I knew where all of it was going, but it was a truth I couldn't reveal. I always figured knowing the future would be fascinating, but suddenly I wasn't so sure.

I should have eaten breakfast before I left because I felt a rumble in my belly. A hot, burning sensation that made me nauseous. My dizziness didn't help the situation either.

"Not sure. My dad wants me to fly over and shoot all the slack happy Nazis I can find, but my mom's real worried. I don't think she likes change... or guns for that matter." He spurted an uncomfortable laugh. "Well, at least it's over there and not here."

"Yeah, that's a good thing... Hopefully, it stays that way."

We turned the corner and headed down the hill, finally getting a glimpse of the old mill. The field looked like a great place for a baseball game, not that anything qualified to the contrary. The barn was taller than a two-story building and looked like it was recently painted a bright red. Such a distinct contrast to the black and white picture I saw in a history book. A single window was near the top looking out over an open field with a beautiful, placid lake off in the distance.

The scene was a mix of contradictions only spring could provide. The buds on the trees provided warmth and color to the area, while the recent frigid nights kept the lake mostly frozen over. I always liked the promise of spring, a nice reminder that something better was around the corner.

The boys had already set up a temporary baseball diamond in the open field. Home plate was right next to the barn with the side of it used as a back stop. Hopefully, they cleared it with the enigmatic Mr. Boomer.

When I stood at home, I was granted a rich view of the lake surrounded by countless budded maples and oaks. A few willows straddled the sides of the lake like modest bookends, stretching over the water to remind me the lake was the main attraction.

The ground sloped toward the lake, so it was not a perfect field by any means. At least it would provide some roll if we hit it hard enough. The grass was damp from the morning dew, but thank goodness there was not a frost to contend with.

All the boys were there and ready to play: Frank, Eddy, Charlie, even Harry. I was told he was usually such a loner, I should consider it a gift if I ever saw him outside the house. It was five on five, good enough to cover the field if everyone was willing to hustle.

"Let's play ball, you cock-eyed meatballs!" shouted that crazy Eddy. Bill warned me about him, but honestly I found him hilarious. Every team has a designated clown or prankster, and with Eddy I suspected there wasn't even a vote.

Bill told me about the time Eddy switched everyone's pants in their lockers right before a big game. I cackled at the thought of heavy-set Charlie trying on small pants, sucking it in so hard to get them over his big belly that his face turned as red as Boomer's mill. Bill said Charlie leaned over and whispered something about all the mashed potatoes and gravy he ate the night before. He had no idea what was going on.

Of course, Coach wasn't too pleased with their shenanigans, making them run laps till the sun went down. It didn't help when Bill blurted that all the exercise would help Charlie fit into his pants. Stopping to laugh in the middle of a punishment only got them more.

It wound up being a heck of a game. It was tied through the bottom of the fifth when I blasted one toward center, almost making it to the lake. Eddy ran as fast as his legs could take him but wound up having to dig through the marshy weeds to find the ball. By the time they relayed it in, I was already celebrating my home run with Bill and my team.

"Man, you've improved since last year!" Bill yelled.

How did he know how I played last year? And which last year was he talking about? Surprise is one of those emotions that can evoke so many different reactions. At that moment, the only one I could think of was to laugh.

Somehow they thought this would be evenly matched teams, but putting Bill and me on the same team was a bad idea. Maybe I had improved since last year.

Bill smashed a two-run triple to left that broke the game open in the sixth. Charlie was on second with me on first, and as soon as I heard the crack of the bat, I was off and running.

"Here I come, Charlie. Get a move on!" I yelled as I caught up to him rounding third. I just about carried him across home plate.

I did some pitching and struck out the side in the seventh. Nobody in the history of Waterville could ever hit my knuckler, especially when I mixed it up with my heat. It fluttered like a nervous butterfly, completely unaffected by gravity.

I don't think they had ever seen a knuckleball before. When Harry struck out with a wild swat to end the seventh, he swung so hard he fell over on his butt. When he picked himself up off the ground, everyone jogged out to the mound in bewilderment.

"How in the cotton-pickin' world of baseball did you throw that pitch, Johnny?" asked Eddy.

"Well, I don't know if I want to give away my secrets, boys," I smirked.

"C'mon..." said Eddy as he gave me a playful jab.

Bill came running over from short, sounding like a freight train. I braced myself. But his flying leap was not something I could prepare for. We both tumbled to the ground. Two loud thuds.

After a playful headlock, I offered to confess. "Ok, ok, I'll tell ya. Just let me go!"

As soon as Bill loosened his grip, I made a run for it. It must have been hilarious to watch as I ran around the field holding the ball in the air while the rest of the guys chased after me.

I heard a curious mix of giggling and yelling right behind me as I turned around to see who was hot on my trail. I could always pick out Bill's deep belly roars, even from across the meadow. I also laughed so hard I had to slow down to catch my breath.

With my watery eyes clouding my vision, I missed a small stump in the ground. I tripped, landing head first and rolling. I was completely unprepared for Bill jumping on top of me. In any other circumstances, it would have hurt. The other guys soon followed, and we became a raucous pile of laughter and boys.

They attempted to wrestle the ball away from me, but I had a firm grip on it like I was ready to throw a changeup. I could feel Charlie trying to grab that ball with all his might, and with his belly resting on my arm, he just about had it.

But as we struggled and grappled for that ball, my mind suddenly wandered. Everything became unexpectedly shrouded by this distant third-person perspective where either I slowed or everything around me sped up.

Am I ever actually granted time when I'm not thinking or worrying about anything? Do I ever completely lose myself in the present, forgetting about the evil twins of past and future? I wasn't so sure. My mind was such a deep, dark place, I would think about things even when I didn't even know it.

Of course, I blamed my non-existent father for that.

Carefree. I've never liked that word. Truly being free of cares is like this unobtainable goal where I run and run and never actually catch it. I may not show it, but believe me, I always care.

I tried to forget about my real dad back home, even though I've tried to flush him from my memory multiple times. He made one bad decision in his life and that was to leave us. Asshole. It escaped me as to why I cared about that man. But I did.

We continued wrestling on the ground, having such a grand old time. I'd say oblivious was a better way to describe us rather than carefree. The sights and sounds of the trees, the lake, and the vast field seemed so distant and inconsequential. We were so wrapped up in our enjoyment, we didn't bother to think about where we were, or when for that matter.

It was why it took us so long to hear the distant cries for help.

Chapter 9

As the ball was almost wrestled away from my tight grip, Bill's right hand suddenly grew cold and stiff like he was giving up on something important. His body swayed from the kicking and nudging of others, but he had clearly lost interest in our wrestling.

My initial thought was he was powerless against my incredible strength, but then I sheepishly became ashamed of my arrogance. I quickly realized there was something wrong. Something horribly wrong.

"Bill, you ok?" I asked.

I tried to stop moving, but Eddy pushed hard against my chest. I fell over on the hard ground just missing the small stump. Eddy landed on top of me, letting out a barbaric yelp. I wriggled free my hands to deflect the loud sound from my deafening ears.

"Hang on, Eddy. Is Bill alright?" I wondered.

I pushed Eddy to my side in the direction of Charlie, and he rolled over from on top of my chest. I slapped Eddy on his shoulder but only to get his attention. He motioned toward me like he was about to shove me again, but he froze in midair.

I pressed myself up in the grass and snapped my head in the direction of Bill. He stared glossy-eyed in the direction of the lake. I tried to hone in on what had captured his attention, but the commotion around me made it impossible.

I suddenly heard a distant shriek. My chest compressed under a sudden heavy weight, but this time it was not from Eddy.

"Bill, what is that? What do I hear?" I asked more confidently this time.

He snapped out of his trance and gave Harry a quick shove to move him out of the way. As Bill rested on his knees, he darted me a distressed look like the sound he heard was the only sound in the world.

He jumped to his feet and threw down his glove in one swift motion. His rapid sprint toward the lake quickly caught the attention of everyone. Out of sheer interest, the wrestling suddenly stopped.

"Bill! Don't go out there. Wait for us!" I screamed.

I sprang to my feet and chased him toward the large lakeside willow. I tried to interpret exactly what was going on, but running on bumpy ground blurred my vision even more than it already was.

I arrived just as Bill started crawling out on the ice. His cleats were still on, either out of haste or to seize some much-needed traction. He crawled on all fours to distribute his weight yet move as quickly as possible. I knew how thin the ice could be that time of year, so I tried to stop him. But I couldn't, I just couldn't.

The silvery ice slowly thinned to a shadowy blackness about twenty feet out. I detected where Bill was headed as I couldn't miss the rhythmic thrashing in the cold, dark water.

The look of panic on the small boy's face was unforgettable. He wore a light brown coat with a small striped cap and was completely soaked from head to toe. His continued splashing only made matters worse. He was seven or eight years old and his straw-colored hair peeked out from under his cap. His dark blue eyes reflected the arctic water, emanating a horror that still sparks nightmares in me today.

As he thrashed in the water, one of his white, wool mittens was still on his right hand. The other one had fallen off. I quickly scanned the area and spotted the lost mitten sitting silently on top of the ice, a few feet to his left.

One of our baseballs sat right next to the mitten, the clear object of his desire. It was the one that Harry blasted in the fourth, but we decided to not retrieve it for risk of breaking the thin ice. I swiftly regretted that decision.

"Almost there, Bill. You've almost got him," I encouraged.

He lay prostrate across the ice and slowly shuffled to get closer. He was about two feet to the right of the boy, stretching out his left hand to reach him.

"Grab my hand! I've got you!" he yelled out.

The small boy continued to thrash in the freezing water with no acknowledgement of Bill's voice. When the other guys arrived, the ice under Bill began to fracture with an ear-splitting crash.

"Bill! Look out!" I swiftly bent down to crawl for both of them, but Charlie reached down and pulled me back in a tight bear hug.

"Let go! I have to help!" I yelled.

"There's too much weight already," Charlie asserted. "It's not safe."

I shot him a look of disgust even though I knew he was right. I tried to wrestle myself away, but his grip around me was like a snake constricting its prey.

"You got 'em, Bill!" encouraged Eddy. I twisted to my side in Charlie's grasp to get a better view of Bill.

The ice swiftly broke under Bill's weight. He fell into the freezing water right next to the boy.

The flailing arms of the boy made Bill's attempt to grab him even more difficult. Bill reached out and held tightly to the boy's left hand but quickly lost grip when the boy swung entirely around. They both lost their balance.

When the boy went under, Bill dove in after him. Four seconds was an eternity when my best friend was submerged in freezing water.

They finally reappeared together, both making loud gasps for air. Bill's arms wrapped entirely around the boy's chest, as if there was no possible way he would let go.

"I've got you!" Bill yelled to the boy. The boy continued to wrestle, smacking Bill twice in the face. Bill barely flinched.

"Way to go, Bill!" the other guys yelled.

Through their excitement, I couldn't help but be ashamed of our own wrestling for the sake of a stupid ball. It suddenly seemed small and insignificant, as if I had walked a hundred miles away from a mountain then looked back. Charlie joyfully lifted his right hand in the air for a split second. I quickly slid under his grasp and jumped on the ice to help.

"John!" he yelled but to no avail.

I tried to walk on a couple of rocks but soon slipped and landed hard on the ice. Luckily, I missed the rocks. After quickly nursing my shoulder, I crawled out and slid in around the other side of the boy. I instinctively grabbed the mitten and ball as I slid past. In one swift move they landed in my pocket. I fell into the cold, slushy water and grabbed the boy's other arm.

At first, the sudden calmness of the boy reassured me as we reached shore. I glanced over at him, but the ghostly look on his ashen face made me turn away.

"Stay with us, kid! We've got you," Bill cried.

His sudden slaps on the boy's face caught me by surprise. The other guys grabbed the boy by the arms and pulled him in, setting him down right below the protective willow tree. Eddy stripped off his own jacket and quickly put it on top of the boy.

I pulled myself out of the water first then turned around to help Bill. He slipped on the muddy shoreline but regained his balance and brushed himself off.

My body shivered uncontrollably and the chattering of my teeth sounded like a stampede of horses. I knew enough to recognize hypothermia was beginning to set in for me. I could only wonder what it meant for the boy.

We dashed over to see how the boy was doing. Eddy tried to talk to him, but he barely responded. His speech became incomprehensible, sounding like somebody mumbling during a bad dream.

"We've gotta get him to the hospital," Bill declared.

The others encircled the boy, uncertain of what to do. Bill quickly pushed himself in and bent down to pick up the boy. His frozen pants crunched as they draped over Bill's right arm. His head limped upon Bill's left.

"Move it, boys. I'm heading to Saint Mary's!" Bill exclaimed as he squeezed between Harry and the massive trunk of the willow tree. "Meet me there."

I could barely keep up with him as he ran toward town. My legs and chest felt heavy and cold, and the world around me was unclear and blurry. My numbness prevented me from feeling my heart pounding, but deep down I knew it was.

I was surprised what my body could do under extreme circumstances. I was always prone to underestimate myself, while I suspected Bill never thought twice about things like that.

The hospital was only a few blocks away, and we arrived at the emergency room entrance in record time. A young doctor greeted us near the door and quickly slipped his hands under Bill's grasp to grab the boy. As he ran him in, the swiftness of the entire staff was amazing to watch.

Color clearly returned to the boy's face, convincing me to feel confident about his prognosis. Bill, however, looked as ghastly as the ice on the lake.

"Let's sit down, Bill. You don't look so good. There's chairs over there." I pointed toward an empty waiting area right next to a large picture window.

We both trembled from the ever-present chill, but a nurse soon offered us blankets and hot chocolate. The first sip shocked my body but soon filled me with appreciable warmth, and a lively pigment slowly returned to Bill's face.

"You know, that was pretty heroic what you did back there, Bill," I attempted to be upbeat. "You should be commended."

"I don't want to be commended! I did what I had to do to save the boy's life. Anyone would have done the same thing."

A few quiet, uncomfortable minutes passed before I responded.

"But you're the hero among us! The rest of us had no idea what to do, how to help. Heck, none of us even heard his desperate cry. We continued wrestling like insensible idiots."

"Ah, don't chew yourself out. I happened to hear the boy first, that's all." He rubbed the back of his neck.

The other guys eventually dropped off our stuff. They sat with us for a while, but I could tell none of them really wanted to be there. Eddy was the last to leave after Bill told him to go home. He intermittently dozed off, and his bobbing head provided some much needed comic relief. Our laughing always stirred him awake, however.

"You're drooling, Eddy. Go home," Bill told him. Most people are never quite sure when humor is appropriate. Bill is not most people.

* * *

I felt a slight nudge on my shoulder. I wiped my eyes and was surprised by a young couple standing in front of us. They wore matching long, grey coats, which was the most colorful thing about them. I swatted Bill's shoulder. He looked up a bit dazed but realized instantly who they were. Through her tears, we both recognized the same dark blue eyes.

"Are you the boys who rescued our son?" she asked.

"We just went out and got him, that's all," Bill answered.

"Well, thank you. We appreciate all that you did."

"No problem. I hope he's doing ok," I confided.

"I think he's doing better," the man stated. "Thanks again."

He provided a gracious wave as they walked over to the other side of the waiting room. I realized I should have been polite enough to ask the boy's name, but I didn't think of it until after they had left. Everyone has a name, and quite often, it's their most prized possession. Valuable because of uniqueness yet ever-present and impossible to steal.

The room became much larger after they arrived. They sat in chairs right across the room from us, only yards away physically but miles away emotionally.

I quickly closed my eyes again and recalled the time my mom lost me in the spacious Montgomery Ward store downtown. Playing hide-and-seek was no fun when the other person didn't know I was playing. Tough lesson to learn when I was only five years old. I had tucked myself under a large rack of women's coats for quite some time. I was so proud of myself for finding such a great hiding spot. Then I started to wonder.

I somehow had the wherewithal to dash over to customer service and tell the manager my mom was lost. The manager chuckled at the thought of it, then made an announcement over the loudspeaker for a child looking for his lost mother. All the clerks thought I was the cutest little thing, at least until my mom dashed over and scolded me for leaving her.

I really didn't know what the big deal was, but she was madder than I had ever seen her. We were separated for twenty minutes. I, of course, had no measure of how long that was to be separated from my mother. Or for her, to be separated from her child.

It was a painfully quiet ride home. But the one thing I'll never forget was the look on her face when she found me at customer service. It was a mix of relief, concern, and emptiness.

I saw the same look that afternoon at the hospital.

* * *

I stirred again, awakened by a loud noise. My memory was cloudy about the rest, but I distinctly remember seeing the squat, bald doctor standing in front of the couple. He wore flawless white scrubs, but the slope of his shoulders deadened the pureness of his demeanor. His arms reached out in helpless support, his head shaking side to side.

I don't recall much of the dad's reaction, to be honest. But her, I'll always think of her. I remember how frail she looked as she collapsed on the floor, enveloped by her husband's arms. Her unbounded screams echoed across the expansive waiting area, yet they felt distant and dampened by the depth and hollowness of the room.

We soon left without saying a word. What could we say? The afternoon appropriately clouded over and light snow began to fall. The silence between Bill and me as we walked spoke volumes about how we felt. Eddy and Charlie came running back to check on us. But as they turned the corner, they saw how we looked and knew instantly what had happened. They turned right back and never got closer than a half block. I don't think any of us wanted to talk much.

As we passed the open field just south of our block, my hand suddenly grazed the forgotten objects in my pocket. I don't know how I missed the wet mitten soaking the front of my jacket. I pulled it out and looked at it one more time. Whether it was reflecting the weather or the mood, it appeared to take on a duller, grayish tone. It was still drenched, but at least the slush and ice had melted off.

I handed it to Bill, thinking for some reason he would know what to do with it. I sure didn't want it. We considered going back to the hospital to hand it to the parents, but neither of us really cared to do that. I actually hoped I never saw that couple ever again.

"Thanks," was all that Bill could muster as he grabbed the mitten from me and stuck it in the front pouch of his jacket.

I grabbed the ball out of my pocket and threw it as far as I could toward the park. My loud holler barely resonated across the field. The ball landed hard and rolled to a stop near some small bushes.

Let some other boys in town play with that cursed ball.

As I made my way to my front steps, I could sense that Bill wanted to say something. I paused and waited.

"See you tomorrow, John," he sighed. He didn't need to say anything else.

I glared into his moist eyes and waited for that wink. It never came.

He slowly walked away, dragging his feet with every painful step. He pulled the mitten out of his jacket and inspected it as he continued down the sidewalk. He tilted his head and held it in the air as if he was trying to get a closer look at the knitted pattern of the grey wool.

A realization struck me like another deep thrust to my cold chest. I couldn't believe I hadn't thought of it before. I knew that mitten looked familiar.

Chapter 10

I sprinted into my house, not certain what I was running from. I swung around the large, wooden bannister and headed upstairs.

"Hey John. Have a good day?" I faintly heard from my parents sitting in the kitchen.

"Fine," I snapped.

I hurried upstairs as fast as my legs would take me. I quickly stripped out of my soaking baseball clothes and threw them on the ground. They were always wet as of late.

I put on some much warmer boxers, placed the box on the bed, then sat down next to it with one leg draped over the side. As the bed angled toward me, the contents shifted against the side of the box.

The box had lost some luster. The cover was much shinier the day before, as I could no longer see my reflection in the varnish. I can't say I was surprised. The day was defined by grey skies and hovering clouds, neither suitable for reflections.

The hinges produced more of a creaking noise, but I also opened it slowly. I stifled a snicker as I let out a quiet argh, inspired by the noise from the hinges.

I always enjoyed role-playing games when I was a kid. Sarah and I used to do that a lot back when we were younger. We've been doctor and patient, husband and wife, knight and maiden, and sometimes even pirate and damsel in distress. All in a day's work, or fun as the case may be.

This time, though, my faint smile was short-lived as I felt a nauseating sense of guilt. Considering the day's events, I was unsure how else to feel. I looked out the window and grasped for a sense of stability and direction. But it never came.

Most of the contents of the opened box were easy to find. A few small items were trapped in the corner, but I could easily pick them out. The hand-sized Bible slid around every time I shifted on the bed.

As I expected, the mitten was gone.

To be honest, I wasn't sure I wanted to see the stupid thing again anyway. But curiosity was such an unrelenting and powerful force.

Alas, it had found a new home. Wherever it was, I was certain it was resting comfortably right beside the muddy ball. Good riddance.

* * *

I surprised myself at how ready I was to wake up and attack the day. Of course, the smell of fresh blueberry waffles certainly helped as well. I'm always a sucker for waffles.

"Hey Mom! Hey Dad!" I proclaimed as I entered the kitchen.

"Good morning, John," my mom said, "I've got another one just about ready for you. That is, unless your father eats them all first."

The kitchen felt warmer than usual. I glanced outside the kitchen window, but the first tree I saw told me it was windy and brisk. I presumed any warmth I felt was the steam coming from the cast iron waffle maker sitting on the counter.

"How are you doing, John?" asked my father. He briefly looked over at me then glanced down to grab his next bite to eat.

Being asked how I was doing was one of those age-old questions where I had to gauge whether the requester really cared. That is, if I had something awful to share, did they really want to hear it?

"You know what, Dad, yesterday was a great day for baseball," I responded. "The whole gang was there, even Harry. Bill and I were on the same team, we both had great hits, and we won! What a blast."

I took a quick sip of orange juice and scrutinized my dad as he shifted uncomfortably in his chair. He switched his gaze between my mother and me, then looked down at his plate.

"What?" I asked, realizing something was up.

"John, your mom spoke with Bill's mother this morning. We heard all about what happened," he sighed. "I'm sorry John. That must have been difficult."

I glanced up at my mom, but she was focusing intently on the waffle iron. The steam rose around her like a mysterious genie escaping a bottle, providing a thin veil that shrouded her face from my view.

It was a small town. She must have known the boy. I was certain she knew the mother, too. From church, from bridge club, from any number of social clubs and dance halls.

Or it was this all-consuming, every parent's nightmare that connected these women in ways I couldn't even begin to imagine. She reached up to wipe her brow as she tried her best to avoid the escaping hot steam. She also wiped her cheeks, including the one that was not facing the iron.

I assumed that running out of the house or yelling at the top of my lungs were not options at that point. But I sure considered them both.

My dad sensed my apprehension, "If you don't want to talk about it, that's ok, John. Just know..."

"No, I do, Dad. I do want to talk about it." I looked at my plate and realized they had made the comfort food for me. "I just... I just thought we had done enough. I thought we rescued him in time. I thought he was going to get better. I... I just never thought he'd die."

Oddly enough, my mind suddenly wandered back to fourth grade. I pictured myself in Mr. Book's class, looking eagerly at him with my legs crossed on the floor. All the kids crowded around tightly with each given a colorful swath of carpet to sit on. Mine was burnt orange.

I was right next to Peter Krass, my elementary school nemesis. He just kicked me for no good reason and my leg was killing me. But I chose to ignore him. I was too busy escaping into the story. Peter didn't deserve my attention, anyway.

Mr. Book sat in his favorite chair, the felt-covered rocker wrapped in a hideous green skirt. He was reading the end of *Where the Red Fern Grows*, and I feasted on his every word. As the story progressed, however, a deep-down, overwhelming sense of rage boiled inside me. I never knew I had it in me. Did the dogs really have to die? As the girls next to me sobbed into their outstretched hands, I was madder than hell. That couldn't happen, it just couldn't.

If I ever wrote a story, no one would die. I promised myself that, and I kept my promise to never forget.

"Well, John, it's not supposed to happen like that," Dad said. "But, sometimes it does. It's very difficult to understand when someone dies, especially someone so young. But the fact of the matter is that we all die at some point. We have to accept that God has a plan for all of us, and sometimes it's different than what we hope for. I don't know what else to say, John."

I have to admit, I have trouble accepting things I don't like. I become restless just wanting to do something. Anything. That engrained stubbornness that I know runs in my family. Both sides, actually.

"I don't really understand, but I guess I don't have to," I reasoned. "It's just... so hard to accept. I wish we could have done more. I wish we had saved him. Bill did everything, actually. Maybe it's just me that's lacking."

"Don't be so hard on yourself, John. You did everything you could."

How did he know? He wasn't even there.

I tried to forget about it all, but my mind always had this undeniable control on me. Death is just not something I'm good at, which is not to say that anyone really is. The finality of it makes me suddenly aware of my own past regrets, present inadequacies, and future indirections. Must be easier if you're the one doing it, but I hope to never find out.

* * *

We headed for church even though I was not really in the mood. I tried to weasel out of it, but my parents would have nothing of it. My mom might have fallen for it, but my dad stood firm.

It was my first time riding in a 1940s automobile. I swore our Packard was a boat disguised as a car as the interior was so roomy we could have fit twenty people in that thing. It was one gigantic seat in the back where I guess I could have sat in twenty different places. The large steering wheel actually looked like it piloted a yacht, and the dials and controls up front looked so retro to me.

"Where the hell are the seat belts?" I barked.

My parents looked at each other, then back at me.

"Aren't you wearing one with your nice pants, dear?" my mom asked. I apparently confused her enough that she ignored my swearing.

"No, not that kind of belt," I muttered, "a seat belt. You know, to keep you buckled down in case we crash. Although, this boat would just bounce off a brick wall for goodness sake."

My dad shook his head and probably didn't know whether to yell or laugh at my mix of odd comments and cynical attitude. I guessed he felt sorry for me, which irritated me even more.

"We won't crash, and we don't have what you call seat belts, John. And no, it would not bounce off a brick wall, Son," he assured.

"Yeah, whatever," I mumbled. They either didn't hear me or chose to ignore me. My mom back home would have been all over me for that.

We arrived at the church parking lot. Many people mingled about, outfitted in suits and dresses, talking and laughing, and all heading in the same direction. I instantly smelled the nearby lilacs. It all coerced me to discover a slightly better mood, whether I wanted one or not.

As we walked along the sidewalk toward the church, the sunlight reflected off the stained glass windows, giving the plain white building an unmistakable ethereal glow. It rested comfortably on a small hill with a tall steeple that pointed toward the vast indigo sky. It was one of those small-town churches that was so quaint and inviting to its members but would abruptly stop the music if a stranger ever entered.

We sat in the back near a family I didn't recognize. Each row was a long brown pew that had an annoyingly sloped back. I think they purposely made it hard and uncomfortable to ensure everyone stayed awake for an hour.

I twisted my collar wondering why in the world my dad forced me to wear a tie. I was 18 for goodness sake. But I scanned the crowd and noticed all my buddies sitting with their families, all honorary members of the uncomfortable necktie club. At least I wasn't the only one.

Bill's family took up an entire pew in the very last row. Bill sat between his sister, Eleanor, and his dad, and he looked like it was the last place he wanted to be.

Much of the service was an utter daze to me. I purposely slid up and down the back of the pew, trying to give myself something to do. I felt like a little kid again, and in a way, I was. With a mix of concern and speculation, I couldn't help but look behind me at Bill now and then. He never returned the gaze.

The pastor began discussing 2 Corinthians, Chapter 4. He jumped right into it, bypassing any friendly greeting, almost as if there was a time constraint. I tried my best to ignore him, but I was wholly unsuccessful. He had me. I was his audience after all.

Death and resurrection, perplexed but not despaired, seen versus unseen. The contrasts were startling, making me curious if I was forced to take sides. But how could I? It's not like death is a choice.

I couldn't help but contemplate what happens when the inevitable death comes knocking. When all choices dissolve into one. The concept of heaven, however large and roomy it may be, felt like this faraway place that someone decided would be good for me. I could suddenly relate.

I wondered if I could select my own personal heaven. Not personal in the sense that I would be the only one there. That'd be boring. What would be the use? But personal in the sense that I would get to choose who would be with me and what would happen.

My heaven would undoubtedly involve baseball, at least a game a day. The makeshift stadium would be filled with the deafening sounds of yells and applause every time I came up to bat. My parents would sit in the front row of the stands cheering louder than everyone else. Sarah would be dancing in the aisles with my every swing of the bat. Of course, the weather would be perfect without a cloud in the sky.

I could also imagine a little boy running near the field. His toothy grin would complement his deep, dark eyes and reflect his newfound, upbeat attitude. He would run around wherever he wanted, never worrying about what time he had to be home. In fact, the stadium would be in his own backyard, so in a way, he already would be home. He would even be pleased to know that his parents would never scold him about losing his mitten.

As soon as the music stopped for the final song, I got up from my seat and headed to the back. I just about knocked over a few old women to catch Bill before he walked out with his family. Right beside the doorway, I gave a slight tap on his shoulder. He turned with an unforeseen jerk and looked surprised to see me.

"Hey Bill, what's up?" I asked.

He gave me a long, drawn-out look. His tired eyes put a damper on his normally cheery complexion, while his slouched shoulders and haggard look told me a lot of what I needed to know.

"Better than yesterday!" he yelped. "I don't know 'bout you, but I didn't sleep too good last night. Couldn't fall asleep, so I...I stared at the ceiling for hours."

"I hope you eventually did get some sleep, Bill. You look like you need some more to be honest."

"Well, that's good to know. Yeah, I did. I counted sheep. The hundredth sheep was too fat so he tripped over the fence. Sounds terrible but the rhythm of my own laughter put me to sleep."

"You're a kick..." I let out a short chuckle but noticed that Bill didn't join me. I had no idea what I could say to help, so I proposed the only therapy I knew. "Say, you interested in throwing a ball around later?"

He twitched his nose like he suddenly had an itch. He glanced down at the ground then shuffled his feet. His weary eyes looked toward me but avoided direct contact.

"Not really," he finally answered.

I never thought he'd turn down a chance to play ball.

"You sure? I'll round up all the guys again. We can head over to the mill and..."

"John, I don't want to play, ok?" he cut me short, "Sorry but just not today. Maybe... some other time."

"Ah, ok. Yeah, let's play another day."

As our families walked out together, I watched our dads coming down the steps side by side and sharing a story. Our moms followed right behind them with Bill's sisters scattered like popcorn nearby.

"Time to go, John," my dad called out, noticing Bill and I down on the sidewalk.

I waved goodbye but felt an emptiness inside like there was something more I could have said. It was like our conversation ended abruptly, even though it didn't.

As we drove away in our car, I focused on the depth of the blue sky. I strained my neck to peer out the window and spotted a lone cumulus cloud directly above us. It almost looked as if it followed us home. Like a large puff of weightless snow that told me so much yet so little. Certainly, there was hope of good weather for that afternoon. Its hue was in such deep contrast to the cavernous sky, and an even sharper difference to the dark, foreboding skies from the day before.

Oddly enough, the cloud had a reassurance to it, like it had been there before and it will be there again. But since it served no purpose, good or bad, I wondered why it even bothered. If I first deciphered why I even cared, I could figure it out.

In all the baseball stories I had heard from my grandpa, he never once mentioned the boy and the ice. As I look back on it, however, the mitten in the box spoke loud and clear.

Chapter 11

Days flew by like a fast-brewing spring storm, and baseball season ended just as quickly as it started. The weather continued to improve even though our offense did not. Beautiful blue skies greeted us so often at game time. Whoever heard of nice, spring weather in Wisconsin? Very calm, too, except for the wind generated by our whiffs at the plate. Come to think of it, the better the weather, the worse we played. With adversity as a catalyst, it was too bad the weather improved like it did.

With baseball season over, I had enough time on my hands to do something I had wanted to do for quite some time. It was the first weekend after school let out, and I could hear the warmth of the air calling me to get out of the house. So, I stopped by Bill's place and asked him if he wanted to head out to a lake with his boat.

"Sure, I'll go. As long as you do the rowing," he obliged without even a pause to think.

Of course, the boat had a motor on it, but it sure was not going to win any kind of race. It was a 10-horsepower that was barely enough to keep going forward. Honestly, I could row faster, but who wants to do that?

"You know you can buy non-wimpy motors that take you around the lake in less than an hour," I kidded.

"Well then I look forward to getting one from you for my birthday."

We strapped his wooden Chris Craft to the back of his parents' Ford and threw our fishing poles in the back for good measure. We headed down to Hahn's Lake not far outside of town, right next to where the Rock River makes a dramatic winding turn back to the north. Actually, the river feeds into the south side of the lake making it a bit murky and weedy in places. But it was great for fishing. My dad suggested it so we thought we'd give it a try. Not a huge lake by any stretch of the imagination, but we knew it would be quiet and unassuming.

We found the public launch on the north side of the lake. Bill skillfully backed up the truck and dropped the boat in without making the darn thing tip over. We threw in our equipment, pushed off from the shore to be far enough from the weeds, then started Bill's potent motor. We were off like a herd of turtles.

I had ridden in boats before, but never a wooden one like Bill's. I thought of it as a cross between Popeye's motorboat and the African Queen. An enclosed area up front for driving the boat, and an open area in back for fishing or just hanging out. It was painted red, white, and blue, a patriotic paint job that would make both George Washington and Popeye proud. To me, it reeked of nostalgia with a heavy dose of character.

Caleb's dad had a big, powerful speedboat that was fun to take up north where a lake was around every turn. Way back in freshman year, we stayed near Hayward for a long weekend where we boated and kayaked until the sun went down. The fish weren't biting, but I quickly realized that wasn't the point.

Even though Bill's boat was small, he and I fit just fine with room to spare for our poles. It had such a deep, low-riding hull, I felt like I was riding a kayak. That was fine with me. I loved the feeling of being so close to the calm water, as if the perspective of closeness suddenly changed my point of view.

"This is an awesome boat, Bill," I remarked. "Where'd your dad get it?"

He turned and unexpectedly gushed. I think he liked being part of a select society who knew what the word awesome meant.

"He bought it about five years ago from an 81-year old fella who lives up on the north side of town. Said he didn't have any use for it anymore. It needed some fixin' up and a new paint job, but now it rides like a champ."

We headed around the east edge of the water, trying our best to avoid the marshes. It was nice to see the ducks and Canadian geese back for their summer vacation.

"Is that a loon over there?" I asked.

"Yeah, it sure is. Well, lookie there," Bill whispered.

We saw it for a brief moment about 30-40 feet in front of us. Before we knew it, the loon quickly dove under the water and eventually re-emerged behind us. He continued his diving sequence until we lost track of where he was.

"Looks like a game of *Where's Waldo*," I pointed out, "Thank goodness he left the red and white striped shirt back at the nest."

"Huh? What are you talking about? Sometimes I don't know about you, kid." He shook his head from side to side.

I don't remember if I said those kinds of things on purpose, just to be different, or if I became careless with slips of the tongue. Perhaps it was wistfulness for my old life, or I just liked to rile him up. If there must be a reason for everything, then I'd consider choosing.

"Oh nothing...This sure is a great day out here." I decided to change the subject. "I'm surprised no one else is out here."

"Fine with me. Nice and quiet."

"So, tell me more about Anna. How long have the two of you been going steady?"

"You don't remember? We met in P.E. during the school year. We've been going steady ever since," Bill answered.

"Oh yeah, forgot about that," I lied as best I could. "She must have noticed you in swim class and was instantly impressed."

"Ah, cut it out," he said as he brushed his hand toward me attempting to give me a push. Good thing I was just out of arm's reach.

I had never seen his cheeks turn such a bright red. Which was not to say he was the only one who felt embarrassed. I tried to forget my swimming encounter as best I could. When I envisioned a list of things I want to do with my life, being buck naked in front of a whole bunch of guys was not even close to making the list.

"Nah, we played volleyball together. She's tops, man. She was the setter, and I was the hitter. The rest, they say, is history," he said.

I grunted. Of course it involved a sport. How else would my grandpa meet someone?

"Hey, we should double date sometime," he added. "She somehow likes you a lot even after everything I've told her. She wants to set you up with another broad. Friend of hers. Not my brainchild, but I kinda like the idea."

"Ah, ok. Why not?" I responded with my lips moving faster than I could control.

"It'd be swell. We could dance the night away then hit the malt shop over on Main." He sounding mysteriously like he'd been planning this out for a while.

"Yeah, that'd be fun, I guess."

I had seen the two of them together at school, and they did make a cute couple. The way they held hands when they walked, the way she leaned into him when she laughed. I could see them together for a long time, which both fascinated and frightened me at the same time. I would never tell him any of that, though. How could I?

We continued around the lake at slightly less than breakneck speed, watching the birds take flight around us. The motor emitted a quiet hum like the muffled sounds of a distant airplane. Bass and walleye jumped out of the water next to our boat. Racing us, and winning. I could reach out and touch them in the air.

We lapped the entire lake twice, checking out possible locations to drop anchor and catch some fish. I was well aware of Bill's world-renowned instincts to find just the right fishing spots, so I kept quiet and stayed out of his way.

He stopped the motor near the east side of the lake, floating us to within about 20 feet of a heavy marshy area. The cattails peeked above the water, and the lily pads were larger than my hand. I suddenly stopped moving. Completely calm. I looked around like I just heard a sound I never heard before. It was nothing, which of course, was everything.

The water looked to be about 4-5 feet deep, so Bill dropped the heavy, rusted anchor. The fish whisperer was clearly satisfied with his choice of locations. Sure enough, only minutes passed before we got our first bite.

The calmness of the water created a perfect reflection of the sun. Blinding but beautiful.

"This is a blast," I proclaimed. He gave me another funny look but let it pass.

"Yeah, I don't get out fishing enough, especially during baseball season," he replied. "Just too busy to do anything else besides schoolwork."

A prolonged silence ensued while I waited for him to elaborate. There is always a certain amount of contemplation that comes from silence, but what I waited for never came.

I wanted an explanation. I needed an explanation.

"So... why'd you quit baseball?"

"I didn't quit baseball!" he yelled. He stared out at his line, waiting for fish that never came.

"Yes you did, Bill! After our game out at the stinkin' mill, you never rejoined the team," I said but then softened my tone. "We missed you in the playoffs, buddy."

A breeze suddenly picked up, creating ripples on the surface of the water. We sat in a protected spot as the thick vegetation in the marsh dampened the waves as quickly as they came. It was a good spot to be in.

"Baseball quit me, John," he finally said.

It was about the last answer I thought he would say.

"What the hell do you mean by that?"

He cleared his throat, making a loud guttural noise that spooked any fish with ears. He continued staring at his fishing pole as if the answer to my question was somehow hanging at the end of the line. In an odd sort of way, it was.

I felt a tug on my line, so I pulled up quickly on my pole. I reeled it in as fast as I could when I saw the large catfish, but I was too late. It got its nibble then swiftly swam away. Left without saying a word. The fish didn't speak either.

"I don't know what to tell you, John," he answered in a much more hushed tone. "My heart left the game after we saw that boy on the icy lake. I... I just had trouble justifying to myself that the game was worth my time.

"Did you know the boy's name was Ben? I read about the funeral a few days later. Actually, don't tell anyone else, but I stopped by the church and sat in the back. It was at that Presbyterian Church over on Fourth by the bakery. I don't think anybody saw me as I slipped out before it was over."

I squinted and tilted my head in his direction, "Why hadn't you told me about that? I woulda gone with you."

For some reason, my initial reaction was tainted by anger. In all honesty, however, I would have never found the courage to go anywhere near that funeral. Never.

"I don't know." He continued staring at his line. "I guess I wasn't sure how I would react so I decided to go by myself. Don't take it personally, I just... I didn't know what to do or how to take it all. But nosiness got the best of me."

"So... how was it? I mean, I assume it was pretty miserable."

"Yeah, it certainly was. I left after his mom spoke. Couldn't take it anymore. Felt like the room was about to explode."

"Sorry, Bill. I can kinda see why it affected your love for baseball." I said it even though I didn't believe it. "It's just too bad you didn't play anymore. The playoffs were coming, and... well, a championship would have been a special thing to share."

"Yeah, it woulda been. But it's tough to play ball when you're carrying around a 50 pound sack of guilt," he reasoned.

"I did miss playing with you, John, but we did play ball together. The muddy game was a once-in-a-lifetime, and the game by the mill sure was special. We whooped 'em, you and me. I just wished it hadn't ended the way it did."

It was a weird sensation, sitting there in the boat hearing him express what I wanted to say but didn't have the courage to.

The experience with the boy at the lake did change things, for the good and the bad of it. What should have been a rallying cry instead became a measure of how much cry we had left in us.

Was it planned? Not at all. But then again, most life-altering events never are.

He continued fishing without ever taking his eyes off the line. I'm sure he didn't want to miss a thing. I actually felt exactly the same way.

* * *

Hours passed before we knew it, and Bill's bucket filled up with bass, walleye, catfish, anything that took the bait. We continued talking about everything from school and baseball to girls and well, more girls. Across two generations and multiple decades, it was amazing how a common language could be spoken. Some people focus on how things have changed over the years. In a few important ways, I beg to differ. There are some things that are just universal and constant. Guys talk about girls. It's what keeps the planets aligned.

Sometimes, though, we just sat there enjoying the calmness of the water. It was just the two of us, and I wouldn't have had it any other way.

It was getting late, so we decided to start heading back. As Bill picked up the anchor, I grabbed the opportunity to enjoy the scenery. The purity of the tranquil water, the large rocks by the shoreline, the marsh, the small beach by the road. I didn't think this lake had changed at all over the years, which was fine with me.

A breeze started blowing and ruffled the nearby leaves, averting my attention. Branches swayed back and forth as I listened closely to the movement of the trees. It reminded me of taking walks in fall surrounded by colorful foliage. Even as a teenager, I always loved being outside when the leaves changed colors. It was months off, but I was already thinking about it. The assorted hues, from green to red, yellow, and orange. Always happens, but never the same way twice. I guess sometimes change is good.

I was the first to see it high up in that expansive oak. Biggest tree around, looking like it boasted its size. I couldn't take my eyes off of the bird, honestly, as the sight of it was simply breathtaking. It was not how I would have predicted it. I didn't realize until long afterwards, this was precisely how I was going to remember that fishing trip with my grandpa.

Chapter 12

"Hey Bill, look up there!" I pointed to the highest limb on the tallest tree, just beyond the marsh. We both strained our necks, twisted and upward.

"Where? I don't see anything."

"Way up there, at the top of that humungous oak."

He dropped the anchor into the back of the boat and stood up to get a better view. The boat swayed from side to side, almost knocking Bill over. He quickly regained his balance, and the boat eventually steadied. He shielded his eyes to protect them from the bright afternoon sun.

"Ah, I see it, too!" he declared. "Man, you don't see that very often."

We both watched the huge nest made of various sticks and brush. The bald eagle looked so beautiful and majestic, enough to take a grown man's breath away. He had a white crested neck full of feathers and a large beak that stood out like he was ready to proclaim his presence and scare away anything that would dare come near the nest. The eagle stood motionless for quite a while, almost as if sensing we were there watching.

I suddenly noticed what gave him the guardianship role that he clearly took great pride in.

"Look at what's popping their heads up, just over the edge of the nest."

Bill instantly saw it, too. We glanced at each other in a look of excitement and awe.

Three helpless babies were just barely noticeable awaiting their food. I could faintly hear their chirps as they openly spoke to us onlookers. They clearly enjoyed the protection of their father. Who wouldn't?

However, like all good things in life, that protection was temporary. One day they would have to be on their own, which was also their chance to fly. Their father would teach them everything he knew, then suddenly push them out of the nest, forcing them to flap their wings in one death-defying leap.

They would get their chance. Not today, but someday. Someday when they least expected it, they would soar on their own.

I admired that eagle. The majestic beast was both a source of food for his young as well as a source of needed protection. Wrapped comfortably by the massive wings of their father, the babies would clearly never be able to survive on their own. They looked to him for everything, and he graciously provided.

Of course, I was also insanely jealous of those eaglets. In a way, I was pushed out of my nest and forced to fly at a very early age. Was I able to fly? Only for survival. Did my father teach me everything he knew? Hell no.

We became oblivious. Again. We watched the eagle for longer than we realized. Somehow, neither of us noticed we were floating toward shore. We became so entangled in the weeds, Bill was forced to tilt the motor out of the water and clean it off. After all that silly talk about rowing, we had forgotten to bring a paddle. I cupped my hands and splashed the water back to try and get us moving. Bill laughed at my feeble attempt.

I could just about reach the bottom of the lake so I threw off my shoes into the boat and jumped out. The water was frigid, providing a compelling reminder that it was ice only a few months earlier. I really didn't need that.

I grabbed the side of the boat and led us into more open waters. The boat was heavy, but I slowly maneuvered it in the direction I wanted to go.

We were soon out of the marsh, so I jumped back in the boat. Bill was just about ready to start the motor when we both heard a loud shriek. The eagle suddenly left his nest and was now engaged in fierce combat with a hawk, another beautiful and massive bird that was clearly on the attack.

The powerful hawk dive bombed toward the eagle, but the eagle stood his ground, or his air for that matter. The hawk lacerated the eagle with his strong beak, scattering feathers across the surface of the water not far from our boat.

The hawk made one more intimidating, departing gesture, then flew away as swiftly as he had come. The eagle chased after him, but only enough to make certain the hawk had left the area. It was only for a brief but harrowing moment that the eagle was away from the nest.

The babies, of course, were completely clueless to what their father had just gone through for them. Little did they know, but their father just saved their lives. They simply chirped away wanting more food. Can innocence or naiveté ever be an excuse for selfishness?

One of the feathers sat right next to the boat, lightly floating on the placid blanket of the lake. I reached over the side and barely grabbed it with my outstretched hand.

I shook off the wetness and held it in the air to get a good look. The pure color and rugged size led me to believe it had come from the neck of the beautiful bird, and the softness of the feather felt nice as it brushed against my hand.

The quill was large and alluring like it could be dipped in ink and used to write. There was even a slight hole at the tip of its sharp base. Somebody could craft a wonderful story with that feather. I was certain of it.

Bill was clearly watching me, so I reached out and handed it to him. He held it tightly in his hand, not enough to damage it but just enough to ensure it would be his. It was with unspoken certainty that I knew he would keep it forever and never lose it.

Of course, I had seen the feather before. I had even held it in my hand and brushed it against my arm to prove its softness. And if the muddy ball and mitten had taught me anything at that point, I knew the contents of the treasured box had been reduced by one.

"Wow! That was amazing," I pointed out. "I don't think I've ever seen such a thing."

"Me neither," he added. "Once in a lifetime, I'd say."

"I loved how the eagle went straight from hangin' out in the nest to fightin' the hawk. I'll remember that for a long time."

* * *

We packed up our stuff in the boat and connected it to Bill's vehicle. He parked the car and suggested we go for a swim before heading back. I agreed as long as he promised to keep some clothes on.

His loud belly laugh resounded across the normally serene lake. The eagle was suddenly on guard, wondering what wicked beast could produce such an uproar.

Not to worry, it was only Bill being Bill.

The water was murky and felt downright arctic, but we went for a quick dip anyway. The lake was shallow for the first ten feet near the shore, then suddenly dropped off to an unknown depth. We gauged it was at least deep enough to jump off the overhanging limb from the nearby massive maple tree. We took daring leaps off the tree to ensure making it past the edge of the drop off, but we both jumped at least ten times without hitting bottom.

After a full day at the lake, it was time to head home. We shivered in our skivvies before drying off with our towels. The rest of our clothes were on in a flash, and we soon headed for home.

"Thanks for invitin' me," Bill said. "That sure was a humdinger on the lake today."

"Yeah, sure was fun." I hoped I was interpreting him correctly. "I haven't seen a bald eagle in such a long time. Not since we fished years ago up on the flowage."

"When did we ever fish the flowage? I don't recall that at all."

"Oh, you will, Bill. You'll love it!"

He exchanged funny looks toward me with watching the road. But I just beamed, coupled with a hearty laugh that was part sentiment, part concealment.

* * *

The beauty of that eagle's nest was there all along, I just needed something to tell me to look up. It was the wind. It rustled the leaves of the tree, which in turn, told me what it knew. Funny how that works. There's a role for everybody, and everybody has a role. Mine was simply to listen.

For me, that day was special in and of itself. But more importantly, it also brought back so many memories from the past that I frankly forgot I had. I was reminded of the fishing trips with my grandpa up north, way back when I was so young without a care in the world. We'd go for long drives in his beat-up Chevy pickup just to arrive at his favorite fishing hole. He would always drive at his own speed regardless of what the authorities had arbitrarily posted as a limit. Driving 30-35 mph on a 55 mph two-lane country road was not unheard of. He definitely took his good, old time and frankly didn't care what anyone else thought.

I grew up thinking that all Illinois tourists were rude, and maybe I was right. Bill always said they drove too fast and were to blame for everything from Packer losses to potholes. I was introduced to some fascinating words and gestures directed toward my grandpa when those drivers finally passed him on the left. He would keep right on talking and ignore those speedsters.

When we finally arrived at that special spot, we spent hours just watching, waiting for something to bite. Anything. Of course, we rarely ever caught anything and much of the time was spent just sitting there enjoying the quietness of it all. I always wondered about his motives as his special fishing holes rarely turned out to be much. At least in terms of fishing, that is.

Looking back on it, those fishing trips took place within distinct events in my life, like bookends on a shelf. They started soon after my dad left. I don't recall much about that time, but I guess he felt like he needed to step in and be a father figure for me.

Unfortunately, the fishing trips ended on my own doing. It was right around my 14th birthday when we went on what I thought was our last fishing trip.

He had great plans for that trip as a birthday gift. But it was like turning 14 flipped a switch within me. My attitude was awful the whole dang trip. The only driving he did in the car was to drive me nuts. We couldn't get there soon enough. Worse yet, he confiscated my headphones and forced me to listen to his regurgitated stories. And it even went downhill after that. I don't remember who called off future fishing trips, him or me.

If only I knew how good I had it.

For Bill, of course, this would be his future. A future he was unaware of, but I knew would happen. The frustration of not being able to share it with him was a lot to carry. I wanted to tell him about what his life would be like and about the wonderful daughter he would raise. And of course, the awesome grandkids he would have.

But I couldn't.

How could I tell him about his future? Would he believe me or think I was downright crazy? By the time the events actually happened, they would simply slip into common knowledge. Unappreciated? Maybe.

So, I couldn't tell him. I assumed he didn't even want to know. But I knew I did.

* * *

"Hey, wanna come over for dinner?" Bill asked. "My sisters are cookin' again!"

"Oh boy, what a treat..." I answered sarcastically. "I'm awfully hungry. I'll eat anything, even your sisters' cookin'."

"Yeah, we'll see what they conjure up tonight. They can't even cook with gas," he chuckled. "Not sure whose turn it is but adventure into the unknown will definitely be on the menu."

"I'd like to stop at home first, unless you want me shivering in my wet clothes. By the way... do you not have a gas stove?"

"Sounds good. I'll drop you off. Cooking with gas is a figure of speech there, Truck. It means to do something right. Man, has that forehead of yours healed yet?"

He turned onto our block and parked the car right in front of my house.

"Oh yeah that. Well, just make sure they prepare enough food! They need to feed both of us, and I know how much you eat."

"Hey, I never met a meal I didn't like, even my sisters'... Sure, I'll warn 'em you're comin'."

I loved how things were so unplanned, so laid back. Back home, I always needed to let my mom know a day ahead of time if Caleb was coming over. 'Always gotta call first so we can clean,' is what my mom would say. I always assumed by we she meant her, because our house always looked peachy to me.

I walked in my front door and heard the faint sounds of the radio in the front room.

"Hey Dad, how was your day?" I took off my shoes and placed them near the front door.

"Great, John." He perked up and looked at me. "Got some stuff done around the house and then relaxed. How was the lake? Catch anything?"

"Oh, yeah, almost forgot we fished today." I walked over to the entryway and leaned against the wall. "We caught a few. Also saw an eagle over by Thompson's place."

"A bald eagle?"

"Yes sir, it was. Neat to see. Babies, too." I extended my hands to indicate how small they were. "Say, do you mind if I eat over at Bill's place tonight? He said his sisters are cookin'."

"Well, gee, you can't miss that. Sure, that's fine. I think Mom was thinking leftovers tonight so no big deal."

"I'm sure that chicken casserole would be great heated in the microwave."

My dad gave me the oddest look, "What do you mean by that?"

"Oh nothing. Sounds good. I'm gonna change then head on over." I had to smile, just to myself.

I ran upstairs and headed for my room, my ulterior motive in focus. I was not sure why I even wanted to look, but I had to check if the feather was still there. The items were vanishing one by one, leaving no trace of their existence behind.

I grabbed the box off my dresser. It was more tattered than the last time I saw it, with rusted hinges and varnish stripped away off the top. It had clearly accelerated its deterioration process.

Thank goodness the key still worked.

I opened the box and heard a louder creaking noise this time. I glanced inside and saw all remaining contents, except the feather. I shrugged my shoulders. As I stood up from the bed, the Bible shifted to the back of the box. I was about to close it when the unfiltered sunlight shone right where the Bible used to be.

I scratched my head, wondering how it could possibly be there. The same white eagle feather I had just held in my hand on the lake. There it was. I picked it up and gave it a quick look over. I brushed it against my arm to remind myself what it was like. The small break at the tip of the quill told me what I already knew. And to this day, it was the only pure white eagle feather I have ever seen.

I carefully put the feather back into the box in the exact same place where I found it. I shifted the Bible to the other side and angled it into the corner so it could no longer slide on top of the feather. It was not a mandatory separation of unlike items. Quite the contrary. I just wanted to know where each one was.

I closed the lid and softly placed it back on the dresser.

But as I thought about it, my excitement quickly turned into frustration. There was so much I didn't comprehend, so much I wish I knew and understood. Why some things disappeared yet other things stuck around forever. It was all a poorly taught lesson if that was what it was intended to be.

I shook my head in disbelief and ran downstairs. At that point, I wasn't sure if I admired the box or despised it. Either way, the passion was strong. It reminded me of things I didn't want to think about, things from my past I didn't see a need to confront. Why some things stick around while others disappear was beyond me.

I couldn't tell Bill about the box, and honestly, there was no one I could tell at that point. It certainly would not make any sense, and he would never believe me anyway.

I headed over to Bill's house, slamming the door behind me. My step suddenly became quicker, becoming a run by the end. My drive was much more than hunger.

I was bound and determined to ask my grandpa a question. One I wanted to ask him ever since I traveled back in time.

Chapter 13

When I arrived at Bill's house, his brother, Donny, and his dad were hanging out in the front yard. His dad was pruning some over-grown bushes, and Donny, who's a bit younger than Bill, was nearby tossing a baseball in the air. Glove in hand, he ran around the yard playing catch with himself. Bill lounged on the front porch waiting for his visitor.

"Come join me, Johnny. Want anything to drink?" he asked.

"No, I'm fine. Thanks," I breathed, ending my short dash from home.

I pulled up a metal lawn chair and plopped down right next to him. He looked mighty relaxed with his feet propped up on the railing and sipping tea like he was on a plantation. He had changed his clothes after fishing and was now wearing a simple, white undershirt and some old, brown slacks that had seen better days.

Their vast, wooden porch was recently painted a nice clean shade of white, and it looked good in front of their cream-colored brick bungalow. However, I always wondered how his family of nine fit into that house without running into each other all the time. That explained why the men were outside.

"You look relaxed," I pointed out, which was more than I could say for myself. My chair was in dire need of a cushion.

"Oh no, I'm quite worried whether my father will trim those bushes correctly." He gestured toward his dad then took a quick sip. "I told him to make 'em look like animals, but he didn't much care for that idea."

He looked at me and grinned.

"I agree. I envision two lion sentries guarding the staircase to your humble mansion."

We shared a laugh at the thought of it. His dad turned and gave Bill a peculiar look, almost like he knew we were snickering about him.

"So, why are you guys out here?" I asked.

"Let's just say the roosters are not allowed in the hen house while the hens are cooking. For some reason, they think we'll crack a joke about their cooking. You know me, I'd never do that."

"Oh no, never." I joined him in putting my feet up on the railing, trying to act relaxed. "By the way, I've got a question for ya, Bill."

"Sure, fire away. Want some pitchin' advice, dontcha?" He motioned his glass toward me then took another sip of his tea.

"No, but I could give you some pointers. That's a topic for a different day..." I was pleasantly surprised by his mention of baseball.

I paused as I wondered how to ask my question without giving away what I knew. I couldn't mention the rugged, old box that he would give me so many years into the distant future. Telling him what he was going to do just might make him reconsider the whole idea. The future was too important for me to consider changing it. The past was, too.

I instinctively rubbed my eye then wrapped my arms around my chest.

"So, you know it's been an eventful last few months for us. From watching the eagle today to... well, even back to the muddy baseball game and your game-winning single."

"Ah, that was a..."

"Yeah, yeah, I know. The blind scorekeeper called it a home run."

It was nice to see him smile about that memory, albeit ever so slightly.

"Actually, even including the game out by Boomer's mill," I added.

His smile left as quickly as it came. He readjusted himself in his chair and put his feet down off the railing.

"Where are you going with this, John?" he snapped.

At the time, I wasn't sure why it was a big deal to me. But it was.

"I guess I'm just wondering... from all those events, you've had a few items that you've kept, as... well, ways to remember what happened. Why do you keep 'em and what do you do with 'em?"

He shifted around again then stared off watching his brother toss his baseball in the air. It convinced me to watch as well. I could tell Donny was trying to throw it as high he could yet still catch it. He was actually getting fairly high, taller than some of the nearby trees. It was a worthy effort, and he wouldn't know unless he tried.

"Well… You know me, I've always loved telling stories. I wanted a way to remember important things that happened, so I just throw 'em in a box in my closet," he said then took a deep breath, "I figure someday they'll be important to somebody somewhere."

He put his feet back on top of the railing then took a sip, marked noticeably by the clinking of the ice against the glass.

"That's neat, Bill." I leaned toward him. "I'm sure somebody will find 'em important. No doubt, somebody real special."

"Actually, my grandpa suggested it to me before he passed away last year. Said he did the same thing when he was a kid. Sounded like a nifty idea so I went with it."

"Well, I think it's a cool idea."

"Cool? There you go again…"

We laughed again. How could we not? We've always miscommunicated on some level, but this was different. However, at some point it wondrously transformed from an impediment to an amusement. One of those things we shared together, just the two of us. No one else really understood, but that was exactly the point.

"Time to eat!" came the holler as Bill's sister, Hazel, opened the door to inform us of mealtime. Her long hair was fastened clumsily into a bun, her thin dress wrapped tightly around her ample body.

Perfect timing as my stomach had been growling ever since we left the lake.

While Bill loved to hunt and fish with his dad and brother, he also grew up with six mothers. At least that's how he liked to describe it. He had five sisters who were wonderful people to have around, but they'd smack his head if he ever got out of hand. Bill told me he actually tried to get in trouble now and then, but we are all drawn to forbidden fruit. As long as his sisters don't prepare the fruit for a meal, that is.

We sat down for dinner around a large table in their dining room. Bill's parents sat on wooden chairs at the ends while the kids and I sat on benches that lined the sides. The table fell somewhere in the spectrum between King Arthur's glorious dinner table and a long wooden-planked picnic table. Most of it had a smooth oak finish, but I was certain the scattered scratches served as lasting memories of family meals and events from the past.

We said grace and dug in. Three large dishes were spread across the middle of the table containing a watery mixed vegetables concoction, lumpy mashed potatoes, and a mystery meat.

In this house, family-style could only be loosely translated as 'free for all.' Pandemonium broke out even before the Amen, or so I heard in front of my shut eyes. Bill and Donny were, of course, the first to grab everything. I enjoyed watching but soon realized I needed to join in before it was all gone.

"Is this rabbit or squirrel?" Donny asked.

"Tastes like opossum to me," Bill joked.

"It's chicken, you numbskulls," Eleanor replied above the sounds of snickering.

I remembered Bill telling me how the Depression was rough on his family. His dad once owned a farm outside of town but couldn't sell his crop to save his life. Or his family's. Luckily, he found a job in town working as a plumber. A lot of customers couldn't pay him too much for his work as money was still scarce.

Bill and Donny hunted in the woods just off Tenth Avenue behind the Anderson's place. Some nights, whatever they caught was what they had for dinner. Every now and then, it actually was rabbit or squirrel, or if they were lucky, both.

"This is actually pretty good, Eleanor. Better than Pearl's humble pie last night," Bill said.

"It wasn't humble pie, it was a savory pot pie," responded Pearl. "Next time... you don't get any."

Bill told me his mom really wanted to instill in her daughters how to be proper cooks and housewives when they grew up. 'That's what women did in those days,' he would say. I could picture Sarah just laughing at my mom if she ever suggested that in our house.

"I thought you did a wonderful job last night, Pearl," their mom added. "We'll be sure to add more seasoning next time, though. That's ok, we learn from our mistakes."

"If that's the case, you girls have learned a hell of a lot over the years," Bill quipped.

"Watch it, Bill!" proclaimed his dad, pausing with a forkful of food raised in the air. He shot his son a piercing look.

Bill kept right on eating while watching his dad out of the corner of his eye. He was a nice old man with a round, inviting face. But no one wanted to be in his dog house. His blowups were legendary in this town.

"Actually, my favorite was the beef jerky from last week. Now that was good," added Donny, taking the discussion one step further into an abyss.

"The only jerky around here is you, Donny," replied Helen. "I'll admit, it was slightly overcooked."

"Hey, hey now. You girls always do a wonderful job," said Bill's mom. "I think we should have Billy and Donny cook dinner sometime! Now that would be a real treat."

"No way!" yelled all the girls in unison.

Bill and Donny just laughed it off. Mostly because they knew it would never happen. His dad kept right on eating, mostly staring down at his plate. I think I saw him roll his eyes at the preposterous thought of his boys cooking a meal.

I sat back and enjoyed the fireworks that only a family of nine at dinnertime could provide.

* * *

When everyone was done eating, the other girls all helped clear the table while Eleanor brought out a fascinating looking cake. She placed it right in the middle of the table. It sat on a large flowery platter with handles on the side and rounded, decorative edges. I swore I had seen the dish before but couldn't place where.

"What's the special occasion?" asked the dad.

"Nothing, really," replied Eleanor. "We just thought we'd try a new recipe. It's a vanilla pudding cake."

"I think you'll like it," added Bill's mom.

It was a multi-layer cake with a generous collection of white icing covering the top. It leaned as far right as most local politicians, making me worry it would fall over when she brought it out. But the sweet aroma filled the room, reminding us that looks aren't everything.

"It smells like a pineapple upside down cake my mom makes now and then," I confessed.

"That's nice, dear. I'll have to get the recipe from her sometime," replied Bill's mom.

"Oh, she hasn't made it in quite some time. She might not even remember the recipe," I added with a slight titter, attempting to cover up my slip of the tongue.

Of course, I meant my mom back home. Bill's currently non-existent daughter. The woman who made the same wonderful cake year after year on my birthday. I requested it so often she doesn't even ask what I want anymore. Beef stroganoff and pineapple upside down cake. I could eat that every day for the rest of my God-given life and never grow tired of that meal.

"I'm looking forward to eating it. Looks good," said Bill.

"That's nice to hear, Bill," Eleanor slowed with a puzzled look on her face. "Is there something wrong? You've never said anything nice about my cookin'."

"Well, it should help wash down that poor bird we just devoured," Bill smirked.

"Speaking of which, do we get milk with this?" asked Donny.

"No! You guys are awful," Jennie snapped.

"Watch it, boys!" added Eleanor as she wielded a large knife in her hand and waved it in the direction of her brothers.

"Eleanor... just cut the cake, honey," said Bill's mom in a calming voice. Always the peacemaker.

Eleanor sliced the cake into generous pieces, and Jennie passed them out. We grabbed the plates and handed them down the rows until we each got one. Before I knew it, the platter was empty and the former cake was now a sum of its parts.

"It's actually not too bad," said Donny, breaking the prolonged quietness of the room. We all enjoyed our portions. I thought it even tasted a bit like my mom's cake, but nostalgia can be the ultimate deceiver.

Out of nowhere, the silence was once again broken. This time by an unexpected and horrifying gargled 'augh! augh!'

Everyone desperately scanned the room. It was an awful noise, like a dog with his head stuck in a bucket of water. A garbled choking. It quickly became obvious who it was. Only one of us was flailing his arms.

"Bill!! Are you choking on something?" asked Hazel.

How peculiar to ask someone. Would they ever be in a position to answer 'yes'?

The girls looked up horrified. Bill's dad sprang into action, faster than anyone had ever seen the old man move. He ran up behind Bill and almost pulled his son out of the chair when he abruptly stopped. Bill threw one hand in the air. The other straight for his mouth.

There was an odd clanging sound as his sisters simultaneously dropped their forks. Like the ceremonial start to a boxing round.

Bill appeared to be screaming as his mouth was propped wide open, but the room was desperately quiet. He hunched his shoulders and leaned forward over the table. His thumb and forefinger pinched together. He leaned further up on his haunches.

I angled my head down to get a better view and suddenly noticed what it was. Sticking straight up against the roof of his mouth like a large tent pole. I blurted a laugh, which only gained me a dirty look from Bill's father.

He grabbed the toothpick and pulled it out.

He hoisted it high in the air with an unexpected smirk on his face. Donny joined me in my subdued amusement. Meanwhile, the girls continued with the same look of bewilderment as if shock became an unseen ghost. Eleanor held a muted gasp like she intended to yell but swiftly covered her mouth. It looked like she slapped herself.

"What in the world is that?" asked Bill's dad.

"It's a toothpick, Dad," responded Donny.

"I know it's a toothpick..." His dad rolled his head from side to side to shake out the frustration. "But what in the Sam Hill is it doing in the cake?"

Everyone glanced over at Eleanor, but she continued to be too disturbed to speak. Her hand still covered her mouth, but her motive clearly switched from shock to shame.

Their mom shook her head and actually started smiling. She reached over and put her hand on Eleanor's shoulder while Eleanor, God bless her, started crying her eyes out.

"They were used to hold the layers of the cake together," revealed Bill's mom as she turned to Eleanor. "I guess we forgot to take one out. Not a big deal as no one got hurt."

"That's one way to get back at me, Eleanor. Clever," said Bill.

"I didn't do it on purpose!"

"I'm kidding, Eleanor. I didn't mind. It only proved how big of a mouth I actually have," responded Bill with an odd mix of sarcasm and reassurance.

Bill's dad returned to his seat and calm was once again restored. Even Eleanor cracked a smile. We all continued eating our slices, and the room was quiet. This time, a different kind of quiet.

"Be sure to put that toothpick in your box, Bill," I pointed and nodded, then crossed my arms. I returned his familiar wink.

Bill placed his elbows on the table, grasped the toothpick out in front of him and clutched it like he was displaying a prized jewel. He gestured toward me across the table, "I just might, John. I just might."

Of course, I knew he would keep his promise.

* * *

I checked the box when I got home that evening. I had to. Looked in every edge and corner and under every remaining object. While the feather was still happy to stick around, the toothpick was nowhere to be found. Even so, I knew where it went.

At the time, I wasn't quite sure why my grandpa kept that silly, little thing. It was so small, so brittle. But now, many years later, it means so much more to me than I ever thought it could. Not because I have it anymore, but precisely because I don't. It's gone. Never to be seen again.

It was as if the unpredictabilities and humor of life were keys to a vast vault I never knew existed. If only I knew at the time how precious and short-lived those fleeting moments would be, he wouldn't have had to keep it. But I need a gentle reminder now and then.

Chapter 14

I sat in my living room, trying to search the newspaper for good news. It was hard to find. Europe was a mess and our economy was still in shambles. What else was new? At least the ads were fascinating. Whoever heard of a gallon of milk for 35 cents, or bread for a freakin' dime? I hastily folded the paper and placed it down on the end table.

I glanced outside. The speckled white frost multiplied in the four corners of the window, providing a circular frame to everything outside. But the first barren tree told me something I already knew. The beautiful show of color was over and done with a while ago. Unfortunately, fall was short-lived and pronounced the coming of another winter. It was almost as if the trees had too much to tell me in so little time. Apparently, an elliptical clock was ticking. Good thing they knew.

I was startled when I heard five quick knocks on the front door, followed up by two more. I recognized that 'Shave and a haircut... Two bits' melody anywhere. Actually, I used it all the time tapping on my desk at school. Runs in the family, I guess.

I smiled at my father then jumped to my feet and answered the door. I knew who it was.

"Hey Johnny boy, whatcha doing tonight?" Bill asked, sporting a mischievous grin. Well, more mischievous than normal.

I was not expecting him to drop by but figured he would. He always did. My dad considered him part of the family, and he was right in multiple ways. Bill had clearly come straight from work, wearing his blue overalls and looking as dirty and ragged as ever. The machine shop must have been busy that day. Either that or he decided to roll around in grease just for kicks.

"Not much, Billy... Why'd ya ask?" I crossed my legs and balanced myself against the door handle.

I, too, had just come home from work, albeit a lot cleaner. I'd been working at the grocery store since school let out. I dazzled them in my interview so they gave me a job on the spot. I can bag groceries and stock shelves better and faster than anyone I know. My mom taught me how. Sounds like an odd, unimportant skill to brag about, but put a muskmelon on top of some eggs and see how quickly a customer becomes irate. This was an important life skill.

"Well, I've been thinkin'..." Bill crossed his arms as he leaned back against the door frame.

This couldn't be good. He never thinks before he speaks.

"I was talkin' with Anna the other day and well... We agreed you and her friend should join us on a date tonight."

He mentioned it way back at Hahn's lake, but I was not about to pester him about it. That was months ago. But in the depths of my mind, I wondered when he would ask.

Honestly, I always thought of the whole thing as being temporary. Eventually, I'd travel back to my normal life, or I'd wake up from a dream, and all would be fine. Whatever the case, I figured it was short-lived. It was any wonder I was reluctant to get too close to anyone.

I thought a lot about my family and friends back home, how much they must have worried about me. I was certain they missed me. They had to. It was eight stinkin' months! I would never say anything about it, though. But that's just me. I always think before I speak.

I considered my options. My instinct was to say no, but my mouth did not cooperate, "Uh, I guess so. Sure. What's her friend's name?"

His body shook from a quick chuckle, which pretty much answered my question. "Honestly, I don't know. I can't remember names if my life depended on it. Isn't that right, Bob?"

"Sure is, Caleb," I said that on purpose. "So... let me see, you don't know her name, but you want me to go out with her?"

"Well, I do know she's a looker," he confessed, "and at school I know her good friends call her... well, they call her 'the warden.'"

"The what?"

"The warden. I don't think it's a bad term, I just..."

"Not a bad term? She sounds like a burly prison guard. A real winner. What is she like 6'3", 240? Let me guess, she always sports a black and white striped ensemble?"

"You're hilarious." He pointed toward me then slipped his hands into his pockets. "Nah, it's just a nickname. She's actually really nice. She just... likes to be in charge, I guess. I respect that independence in a woman."

I rolled my eyes. He was getting way ahead of himself, almost as if he was living in the wrong generation. Wait, no, that would be me.

"Sure, I'll go," I quickly answered, my head angling to one side like I was stretching my neck. I surprised myself, not even taking a second thought.

"Great! Be back to pick you up at six." He headed out the door, and I watched him stroll down the walkway. His fingers snapped to a noticeable beat. His own beat, I'm sure.

At the time, I thought I was crazy. Going on a date with a woman I'd never met? Named the warden? Like she'd beat me with a billy club and send me to solitary confinement if I tried anything funny.

I soon realized it was one of the best decisions of my second God-given life.

* * *

I threw on some khaki pants and a crisp white dress shirt. I even voluntarily added a tie. The herringbone sport coat I discovered in the closet looked great with it, so I slipped it on and admired my dashing self in the mirror. The coat slipped on nicely and was a perfect fit. I sure was going to need it as it was a frigid December evening.

"Bill's here, John," my dad yelled up the stairs.

I ran down the stairs, catching myself as I slipped on the last step. While they looked good, those Argyle dress socks were slipperier than I thought.

"Watch yourself," warned my dad. He was waiting at the bottom of the stairs doing his fatherly duties. I think he had forgotten I was 18. "Where you guys going?"

"Not sure. Bill has it all planned out. God help us."

I sat down on the dark wooden bench in the foyer trying to throw on my shoes.

"You have fun, John," my mom added, peeking in from the living room.

"I'll certainly try," I answered while finally lacing my last shoe. "I'll see ya later. Have a great evening, Mom and Dad."

"Don't be out too late, Son," yelled my dad as I dashed out the front door. The other proverbial dad thing. One I could not tire of, however.

A biting wind grabbed my attention as I ran down the front steps toward the car. I was thankful I had shoveled the light snow earlier in the day or else the walkway would have been icy. Besides the wind, it was actually a beautiful evening. Snow perched daringly on the entire lengths of the tree branches, giving them a silvery silhouette like a shadow projected on itself.

I hopped in the front passenger seat of Bill's black Chevy and quickly closed the door. It made a loud thud, but at least I knew the cold air would stay outside. I instinctively reached for the seat belt, which of course, was not there. I never got used to that.

"You look spiffy there, Johan. Ya ready?"

"You don't look too shabby yourself, ya big stud. I'm ready..."

"Here goes nothing!"

We first drove over to Anna's place. She lived on a farm about three miles outside of town. While the barns were old, the house looked recently renovated. I think the driveway was just as long as the roads to get there, so I was happy when we finally arrived. Bill was getting tired of my fingers tapping on the dashboard. His Chevy surprisingly plowed right through the snow accumulated on the driveway.

Bill kept the car running and went to the door to greet her like a gentleman. I hoped he wouldn't fall in the muddy snow as he was looking snazzier than I had ever seen him. The pinched-front Fedora, the thin, black tie, the striped shirt, the pleated pants. He really was a big stud.

They came out together a few minutes later, Anna's hand wrapped tightly into Bill's folded arm. Anna wore a navy blue dress protected by a faux fur coat draped around her slim shoulders. I crawled into the back to make sure there was room for everyone.

She slowly slipped into the passenger seat. "Hey John." I couldn't help but notice the overwhelming rush of perfume, like I had just stepped into an invisible, scented cloud. I tried not to gag.

She clutched her hair trying to keep it in a tight bun, but the wind was not cooperating. I had not seen her in a while, but she looked as stunning as usual. No wonder she had been the talk of the school, and Bill loved the attention. Can't say I blamed him.

Whether it was out of jealousy or for other reasons, I held an unexpressed dislike for her. I leaned forward from the deep backseat.

"Hey, Anna. How are ya?" I small-talked as Bill walked around to the other side of the car.

"Good but freezing. It's really cold out there."

"It sure is." I actually agreed with her, I just didn't whine about it.

Bill drove off, the tires sliding on the slick driveway as we started. We headed around the corner to pick up the other gal. I also took the role of the gentleman in stride, heading up to the house of the warden. It felt rude not knowing her name, but I figured it would be ruder to ask.

It was a smaller two-story with a long, narrow concrete walkway leading to the front steps. They, too, had recently shoveled in expectation of our arrival. The front door opened suddenly, and she stood there in a confident stance with her arms at her side. She was about a foot shorter than me, but she didn't care in the least.

"How are you, John?" She barely waited for an answer as she turned around and marched back to the closet to grab her coat.

"I'm great. Can I, um… help you with that?"

I hesitated to go in. When I realized I should run in to help her with her coat, she already had it slipped on. As she started walking toward me, I finally got a good look at her.

She was pretty, but in a tomboy sort of way. She had shorter auburn hair and bright blue eyes. Her face was tender and reassuring like she took pride in her flawless complexion. But that was the only ladylike feature about her. She wore a simple, long-sleeved evergreen dress, but she tugged at the sides and walked as if she didn't like it. I got the feeling she only wore the dress because the era, or her mother, requested it.

"Off we go," she declared as she strode past me and down the steps toward the car.

She kept a fast gait as I struggled to keep up. I walked a few steps behind, pondering where I could have possibly seen her before. Her looks and demeanor felt very familiar, but I couldn't place where I knew her from. Must have been at school. I was certain we had a class together. There was no way she'd tolerate a constant stream of homemaker classes.

As we neared the sidewalk, I dashed around her so I could grab the car door for her. She reached out to grab it herself, not wanting to wait for me apparently. Our hands met on the door handle, and I could sense the awkwardness she felt.

"I'll get it," I said.

"Ok," she mumbled.

She slipped into the back seat, so I closed the door and hurried around to the other side to sit next to her. I just about needed a running start to close that hulking door in the gusty wind. They sure don't make cars like they used to.

She was already interrogating Bill on where we were going.

"Oh, you'll find out soon enough," he replied with a sneaky grin.

She adjusted her dress and shot a look out the window with a quick turn of the head. She was clearly not pleased with the answer. I looked over at her, wondering how in the world she and Anna ever became friends.

* * *

We arrived at our first destination. Knowing Bill, I should have guessed where we were going. It was a Saturday night, and the parking lot was packed with cars. Who wouldn't want to go dancing, especially with the frigid weather outside?

Drinking and dancing would certainly warm even the coldest of souls, especially for someone like me who had never been of legal drinking age before. Apparently, I had instantly transformed into an adult as the legal age back then was 18. Actually, I was surprised I didn't pick up drinking after my dad left, but then again, I was only four at the time. A tad too early to start.

We walked into the Elks Lodge and spotted half the town nestled into a single expansive room. The dimmed lights made it appear shadowed and moody, but the oak paneling gave it a log-cabin feel. The tables were located in half the room and were packed with people intent on filling the room with a cloud of smoke and an aura of commotion. In the other half, the band was already getting into it on a large stage perched above a vast wooden dance floor.

We eventually found an open table way in the back. We placed our coats and purses in the middle of the table, and Bill and Anna headed directly to the dance floor. I raced around the table to pull out a chair for the warden, then sat down right next to her. We both angled our chairs to face the dance floor.

Bill and Anna jumped right into the thick of it, and it was a blast to watch. They appeared to know exactly what they were doing, which made me feel even more awkward and out of place. The deafening sounds of the band swamped the far corners of the room, matched only in style and substance by the rhythmic movement of the dancers and the unmistakable scents of smoke and sweat.

I tried to ignore the long, awkward silence between the warden and me, but I had to chat with her. She was my date after all. I was never good at small talk, but I knew I had to break the ice somehow. 'Here goes nothing,' I said to myself.

"That looks like a blast." I pointed towards the dance floor. "What dance is that?"

"It's the jitterbug," she answered curtly. I waited for her to add 'you moron,' but surprisingly it never came. Hanging out with Bill made me expect novel responses.

I shifted unsteadily in my chair. Swing and a miss.

"Do you come dancing a lot?" I asked after considering my options.

"No, not usually."

Every baseball player should have a strategy when he's down 0-2 in the count. I, on the other hand, did not.

As we sat there, I grew fascinated with the gyrations of the dancers. They were flying all over the floor, and the flailing arms and shaking legs made me think there was little if any inhibition kept in check. I guessed the drinking had already started.

I was captivated, but it was clear only one of us wanted to dance. I glanced over at her and figured I had one more pitch to swing at.

"So how did you and Anna meet?"

"We bowl together."

Of course, bowling. This was the 1940s, and this was also Wisconsin. The bowling capital of the free world. An alley or bar – sometimes both – on every corner. Often times, the crappy weather left no choice but to bowl. Which was not to imply bowling was a last resort activity, at least to the hearty faithful.

"No way! I love bowling. What's your average?"

"Last I looked it was around 180."

"Holy cow! You must be pretty good. Much better than me, I can tell you that."

She gushed like she was just called the prettiest girl in the world.

"I bowl in a few leagues, actually," she confessed. "My dad taught me to bowl when I was five, and I've bowled ever since."

"We'll have to bowl sometime. That'd be fun. If I'm not playing baseball, I'm either bowling or golfing."

"I love golf! My dad taught me that as well. I go out and play whenever I get a chance, at least when the weather cooperates. My favorite course is Brown Deer over in Milwaukee. Challenging but good." I sensed her shoulders loosen as she angled her legs toward me. "My mom always wanted me to be a girly girl, but that was never me. Throw a club or ball in my hand, and I'm happier than a clam. Sports are my thing."

It's funny when I'm with someone I don't know, as it can be a struggle to find things to talk about. But everyone has a passion; I just have to dig deep enough to find it. A comment here, a question there, and lo and behold I've struck gold.

"You ever hit a hole-in-one?" I asked. "I came close a few years ago, but it hit the bottom of the cup on a fly and bounced 20 feet in the air. Unluckiest thing you'd ever see. I swore up and down the whole way to the green."

She swept her head back and simpered as if she suddenly liked me. She leaned forward and crossed her legs in my direction. I suddenly smelled a hint of perfume. "Funny you ask as I just had one last year! Hole #7 at Brown Deer, actually. I jumped up and down and hollered for ten minutes!"

"No way! That is so neat."

And she told me the whole story. From the wind conditions to the details of the course to her strategy on how to maximize distance with improved timing and a looser grip. To think, a looser grip! She also explained how she focuses intently when she bowls. Ignoring spurious chatter, concentrating on consistency, and using her hook to maximize her pin action.

Oh my goodness, I was in love.

"Say, you wanna dance?" I asked as if courage had just become a hot commodity. There was more jitterbug on the dance floor, the only dance anyone seemed to do. Looked like a blast even though I had no idea how to do it.

She held out her outstretched hand as an unvoiced answer of 'yes'. I leapt to my feet not wanting to let the moment pass. She appeared uncertain and tentative, yet willing and deliberate. I wasn't sure if she had danced much before, let alone been on a date with a wonderful gentleman like me. We'd learn the dance together.

We maneuvered to the edge of the dance floor then grabbed both hands and faced each other. I gifted her a huge grin and she tentatively returned it. The quick steps were relatively easy to learn as they were mostly to the beat of the thunderous music. Lots of twisting and twirling with random bouncy leaps as if the floor was on fire. We inadvertently bumped into each other a few times, but I didn't mind. Other than that, we flailed our arms back and forth and up and down, uncertain of what exactly that part involved.

After seeing others do it, I let go of one hand and lifted the other one high in the air. She figured out what I wanted her to do, so she spun around as quickly as she could. As her dress took a wide outward spin, one of her shoes caught on the floor forcing her to lose her balance. I held on tightly and caught her in my arms. The smile she flashed me was priceless.

I glanced across the floor and caught Anna and Bill observing us. How long had they been watching? He tipped his Fedora in my direction and gave me an approving wink.

We danced for hours into the long evening. All the spinning and turning was so much fun yet entirely exhausting. I lost the tie halfway through and hoped no one noticed how sweaty I was. The place had become warm and dark, and reeked of wanton dancers fully expressing their innocence. And I was in the middle of it.

As I looked back on that evening, I realized it was a form of blissful ignorance.

* * *

We eventually left the lodge and headed across the street to the malt shop. It was also crowded with folks, many I recognized as just coming from the dance hall. A popular combination, apparently. The place was long and narrow with booths hugging the outside windows and stools along the counter in the middle.

I spotted a booth toward the back, so we headed toward it and settled in. Bill and Anna sat on one side, and I let the other gal scoot in first on our side. I could sense Anna was worried about getting her fur coat dirty, as she took it off and carefully placed it on the seat next to her.

The entire place looked so retro to me. The shiny blue padding on the seats reflected the bright fluorescent lights. The floor was covered in black and white checkered tiles while the walls were decorated with various Coca-Cola memorabilia. I faintly heard the jukebox playing a song, barely audible above the commotion. The menu was presented on a chalk board behind the counter, and we scanned it to see what the options were. There weren't many, which was fine with us. It was short and sweet.

"You wanna go ask the jerk what the special is today?" Bill asked me.

I looked around and laughed, wondering who in the world he was referring to. I looked back at him, squinted my eyes, and stretched my neck out in a look of confusion. "Excuse me? Who are you calling a jerk?"

Anna giggled but her friend added, "The guy behind the fountain. He's the soda jerk because he jerks the handle. Whom did you think he was referring to?"

"Nobody really. I just thought you were insulting someone, and I sure hoped it wasn't me."

"Oh, I'd tell you if I was insulting you, John. Don't worry about that," Bill assured me, chuckling loud enough for everyone to hear. I laughed with him, just long enough for everyone to think I was playing along with the joke.

I stood up and ordered our Coke sodas from the guy wearing the funny white hat behind the counter. I refused to call him a jerk. Seemed like a nice enough fellow.

I sat on a swiveling stool and watched him add a scoop of ice cream to the four mugs he lined up on the counter. I never got used to the idea of a soda containing anything besides pop. But it sure was tasty. Coke rushed into our mugs as he yanked down the large, metal handle. A layer of foam covered the tops of each.

To think we had to ask someone to help us pour our sodas. How odd.

I paid my 20 cents, grabbed all four mugs by the handles, and placed them on our table back at the booth. We each selected one.

As I sat down, I glanced at the girls, "So, I hear you ladies bowl together?"

"Yes, we do," Anna answered, "Although I'm not very good. She's the one who's really the star."

"I bet I could beat you with both hands tied behind my back," insisted Bill.

"That's a laugh! I'd love to see you try…"

"Bill, I don't know. You haven't heard how good she is," I proclaimed in her defense.

My drink was beginning to turn a milky white before I remembered to take a sip. I watched her out of the corner of my eye. She was not hiding the fact that she was smiling in my direction.

"I have heard, actually. She's the talk of the town," said Bill. "Even more reason for me to beat her."

Funny how my recollection of that evening is now in third-person. I can picture myself wearing a brown sport coat and sitting in a booth with Bill and the two ladies. My view is from across the street, standing outside and craving warmth. We all had our elbows on the table, eagerly leaning in to chat. Every now and then we each took sips of our delicious sodas. The taste was whole-hearted and sweet like a distant memory from a faraway time.

In a way, it was all so short-lived and temporary. But in others, it became much more permanent. The fact I can write about it now solidifies that truth.

* * *

Not until we dropped her off at her house did I realize who she was. I went around to open her door, and I faintly heard Anna say, "See you, Arlis."

Arlis. I'll never forget a name like that.

I stared at her in amazement as she stepped out of the car. I was entranced in thought to other whiles, to other places. I nearly closed the car door on her hand.

She turned around and waited for me to walk with her. I remember how soft her hand felt in mine as I attempted to warm us both against the biting wind. Her head leaned in against my chest. I tried hard to not be rude, but I couldn't help but stare.

I was shocked I hadn't figured it out earlier, but I eventually forgave myself for that. She looked so different than when I last saw her. She had been much older then, but just as spunky as she was that evening.

We reached the top of the stairs. I didn't know what to say, but I did know what I wanted to do. I embraced her across the depths of time, pulling her in close to where and who I was. I wished I could have held her forever. To be given the opportunity to enjoy her another time was beyond words. The alluring sight of her evergreen dress dusted with snowflakes, the subtle hint of perfume that I could only smell if I got close, and her glinting, reflective eyes that I gazed into and saw myself.

I finally recognized the house. My mom had given Sarah and me a tour of significant places in town, and this was one of them. I promised to keep in touch, and left more abruptly than I had planned. Partly because I didn't know how to react.

Halfway down the sidewalk, I turned around and gave a slight motion of my hand, "Goodbye, Arlis."

"Bye, John. It was wonderful seeing you again," she yelled from the doorway with a distinctive glow of light behind her. I watched her as she slowly closed the door.

I wiped my eyes as I descended the final steps, leaving her and re-entering reality. I was stunned. But I was thankful that it happened, not unhappy it was over. Or at least, that was what I convinced myself over and over again the entire ride home.

It took me awhile to recognize the importance of that evening. And it was important in many ways. Of course, what happened was amazing. The dancing, the soda fountain, seeing her again. Events that will always be there, never to disappear, never to be lost.

But the other part was what happened afterwards. A boundary to create definition. Bookends to create a span of time. Precisely why I got lost in moments but wrapped up in memories.

While it was truly a wonderful evening, Bill later called it the end of innocence.

I think he was right.

Chapter 15

When we headed for church the next morning, it was a blustery day in the 20s. The wind howled and the trees shook as if they were nervous. Mostly cloudy with light snow in the forecast. Normal weather for December, no matter what year it was.

Seemed like the entire town was at church that day, a strong showing for a sleepy winter morning. Bill and his family took up an entire row up in front, while I also spotted Eddy and his family way in the back. We arrived late and were forced to sit off to the side with a partially obstructed view behind the pillar. The place was packed.

Apparently, everyone has something to pray for, and sometimes we're even aware what that actually is.

For some reason, I recall insignificant details about that day: misplacing my shoes while getting dressed in my Sunday best, the organist missing the last note of the hymn while the choir kept singing, and how my dad and I almost forgot my mom when we left after church.

"Thanks for remembering me," she muttered as she came running into the car. "By the way, what do you boys want for lunch?"

My dad made a sharp right turn onto Cutler, enough to make the tires squeal. I thought it was cool, but my mom held onto the door handle for dear life. It resulted in the worst dirty look I had seen from her, and surprisingly it was not directed at her teenage son.

"Mind if we eat in the living room?" my dad asked as he pulled the car into the garage. "John and I were hoping to catch the Cardinals-Bears game on the radio. How about something simple like sandwiches?"

"The winner plays the Packers next week," I added. "Should be a heck of a game."

"That's fine with me," my mom said. "I'll put something together quick. Just be sure to change first so you don't spill on your nice clothes."

I was more than happy to oblige. I changed as quickly as I could then ran down the stairs and leapt into the dull red armchair across from my dad. The radio sat on the table between us, and he was already adjusting the dial to find the game broadcast.

I loved the look and feel of that old-fashioned radio. The enormous size of the rounded, wooden case with matching metal dials for changing the volume and frequency. I always had to adjust the frequency dial ever so slightly to tune to the station I wanted. Even then, there was always static. The decorative, swirled openings for the front speakers always looked like stained glass to me. Ironic since the radio served as our football cathedral.

For a while, I had such good memories of that radio, including all the music and shows my dad and I listened to together. He always loved Louis Armstrong or Tommy Dorsey, while I couldn't wait until Jack Benny or Fred Allen came on in the evening. Listening to their comedy routines would make me laugh so hard I'd cry. To me, it became much more than just a radio.

"Great game so far, Dad," I remarked. "Who do you think's gonna win?"

"Well, I don't know, the Bears have such a good offense. You can't beat Luckman."

"And you know, McAfee's not that bad either," I responded with a sly grin, "but he's not even close to Don Hutson. That guy's amazing."

My dad just smiled.

I surprised myself with my 1940s football knowledge. Normally, I keep up with the Packers no matter what, and that season was no different. With the immortal Curly Lambeau as their coach, the Packers tied with the Bears for first place that year. And what a year it was. Not only was it a blast to listen to, it also gave me something to chat about with my dad and Bill.

Of course, anyone who follows the Packers also has to keep track of the Bears. End of discussion. Always important to know where my enemies are.

Somehow, I can still summon the details of that game. The Cardinals took an early lead, but then the Bears came back to tie it at 14 all. Right before halftime, the Cardinals kicked a field goal to take the lead again.

As the second half was about to start, I can still remember everything so vividly. My mom had just entered the room to clean up our plates, and my dad had just come back from the kitchen with a glass of water. I was sitting with my legs crossed on that dull red chair. I'm positive my legs were crossed, left over right.

I took a sip of water and put my glass down on the table.

I then took my last breath of peace.

They interrupted the broadcast for an important announcement: the Japanese had just attacked Pearl Harbor.

The announcement was so short, so abrupt. It came and went so quickly, yet lingered for so long. It was like the acoustics of the room had suddenly changed, and an echo was bouncing back and forth with nothing to stop it.

As I look back on that moment, I cannot for the life of me figure out how I didn't catch that ahead of time. I knew it was 1941, and I knew it was December. But I've forgiven myself for that. Sometimes, even when I think I know something, I can still be taken by surprise.

The plates shattering on the wooden floor was a shocking crescendo to the entire moment. My mom felt terrible about that, and she spent an awfully long time cleaning it up. I suspected it was her way of righting a wrong, however insignificant it was.

It was the first time I had seen my parents embrace. The muffled cry in my father's arms was enough to tell me how much it bothered my mother. She was the one who figured out what it meant for us, or for me in particular, before the rest of us. Or at least, she was the one who showed it.

My father's reaction came in stages. At first, of course, he played the role of comforter. He held my mother tightly until she was able to stand on her own. He played that role well as I don't know what my mother would have done without him.

Then, he gave me that fatherly look of concern, like I was just heading out late at night with friends. He wanted me to be safe. Every father has it. The bouts of worry come with the territory.

Some kids found that annoying, but I felt otherwise. It might be cliché, but I truly didn't realize how important something was until it was taken away from me. If that was the case, then having a father in my life was pretty damn important. The tireless provider, the ever-present mentor, and the fearless protector. So many hats for one man to wear.

He didn't say much, but he really didn't have to. Mainly, he was just there, which was fine by me. Someone to share football games with, someone to bounce thoughts and ideas off of. I admit, I have a knack for not getting along with some people now and then. But even worse are people I don't know but should. Like people who leave. I despise them.

My father's last stage was difficult to describe. We sat for a long time listening to the radio afterwards. His only movements involved reading the paper and drinking water from his glass. I hoped for his sake there was bang-up news to be had in that paper. Not many times we're afforded opportunities to know when something good is about to end.

The second half of the football game made way for other shows, other avenues for escape. It was a good game with an exciting ending, but excitement was, of course, a relative term. His complete silence baffled me at the time. That was, until he broke it in half.

"I just don't get it, John," he finally said.

"What do you mean? The Japanese don't like us, just like the Germans. They had to do it," I answered.

"No, not that." He paused, then proceeded in a near whisper. "How could an enemy in a land so far away disrupt our lives so much here?"

I didn't have an answer, which was not to say he expected one. His question just hung there, like a passing storm cloud that came and went with a distinct purpose.

* * *

I soon headed out for some fresh air, hoping to hear someone else's perspective. As I took the first step onto Bill's porch, I heard the loud, unmistakable voices inside. And it was pretty clear what they were arguing about. I was about to knock when Bill came storming out. The screen door almost slapped me in the face.

He plopped himself into a chair and crossed his arms in a huff.

"Hey Bill, what's new?" I asked.

His body jerked back as he pivoted his head quickly in my direction.

"Hey, John. I didn't even see you there."

"Everything ok in the Kuess residence?"

"Oh, just peachy..." he answered with a deep sigh. "My parents just don't get it."

"Get what?" I sat on the railing, placed my hands on my knee, then faced him directly.

"The whole damn thing! They either think it'll pass right over and nothing will come out of it, or... or they don't want me to get involved."

"How do they know what's going to happen?"

"They don't! That's part of the problem."

But I knew. It was like an uneven path on the sidewalk that lay before me. Bumpy and annoying, but only until I realized it was temporary. Then, it became infuriating.

I don't think it helped me process the day's events, though, or those of any upcoming days for that matter. Knowledge does not always provide me peace of mind. I knew of the upcoming loss and sacrifice, the incredible impact on every family I knew. Many would lose sons, brothers, and fathers. Sometimes, all of the above. Knowing and living it was becoming a lot for me to bear.

"To me it's obvious," he continued. "We'll all be at war before you know it. Every man, woman, and child. Of course, only the men will go to fight, but make no mistake, everyone will get involved. This is going to be an all-out, bloody war for the ages. You can trust me on that."

And I did, I did trust him.

"I thought your dad would agree with you on that?" I moved to the chair next to him. "Seems like a no-nonsense kinda guy who would want to retaliate."

"I thought so, too. But apparently push came to shove. He didn't like it being in his own backyard."

"But Hawaii is so far away. It's not his backyard."

"That's not the backyard I'm talking about... By the way, how did you know about Pearl Harbor?" his chin snapped back into his neck as he squinted right at me.

I had no idea what to say. I had hoped he wouldn't remember that. It was an uncomfortable feeling knowing something I shouldn't.

"Uh... I don't know. A premonition, I guess."

A light snow began to fall as we both watched in a prolonged silence. We both felt awkward for a number of different reasons. Somehow, time passed painfully slow yet exceedingly fast in a confused mix of existence.

"You know, maybe he's right. We shouldn't get involved, or at least you for that matter," I retorted, almost possessively. I rubbed my eye and instinctively folded my arms.

He turned toward me with a cold stare that had nothing to do with the ever-increasing falling snow, "What the hell do you mean by that? You're becoming as soft as my parents, John."

I had become a softie. But I had become a man who knew what he wanted and what he didn't. I was on a tried and true mission to change my family's past, even though I didn't even know if that was even possible.

"I... I just don't think it would be a good idea to head off to some far away land to fight someone you don't know, and... and the machine shop needs you! Can't you request a waiver as a necessary employee?"

He looked at me and started to chuckle. "That's the dumbest idea I've ever heard. Why would I wanna do that?"

"Well... you just need to."

He shook his head. "Sometimes I don't think I know you, John. Your priorities are all whacked out like you live in some kind of dream world."

And he really didn't know me. My quiet demeanor always masked my fierce competitiveness. It was times like that when I considered it necessary to win. I impressed myself at the time with my creativeness, and I knew what I had to do to get what I wanted.

But I misjudged things in so many ways. It was both creative and foolish at the same time. It was not ideal nor was it right. And it was not until much later did I realize that it was not a game, and hence, there really were no winners or losers.

I also knew war was different. Very different.

Chapter 16

"You sure you wanna do this?" I turned toward Bill as we both stood in our entryway. My arms extended out like I was reaching for an answer.

It was clear to me his pig-headedness was on display as I had no chance of talking him out of it. What wasn't clear to me was whether I actually inherited that trait as much as my mom said I did. I sure hope not.

"Yup, no better time than the present," Bill answered. "She won't ever expect it."

I had no idea if Anna actually would be expecting the ring. He held it in his hand and observed it for an extended length of time. He had sold so much of what he owned to save up as much money as he could, and he spent it on the one thing he was holding.

I was certain he knew what heading off to war meant. It was the lingering question of survival that haunted every man who would go overseas. But I was uncertain if he was tying up loose ends before his inevitable demise, or if he was planning out the life he wanted when he returned. Honestly, I'm not sure if he knew either.

Bill knew in his heart what he needed to do. And being the stubborn fool that he was, he was bound and determined to do it. It was his one shot at normalcy, and he wasn't going to let it pass him by.

I wanted to tell him I had such mixed feelings about the whole thing. I saw how he loved spending time with her. How they smiled at each other, and how they stole the show at every dance floor they went to. But I knew who she was as well as who she wasn't.

He was wearing his Sunday best. His starched white shirt was perfectly creased and the straightness of his slender black necktie would be approved by any army squadron commander. He looked like he was ready for battle.

"Do you mind driving me over to the Petersons?" he asked.

"Ah, sure. I'd be happy to!" I responded, hoping I was doing a good job of suppressing my apprehension.

I suspected he was just looking for moral support, or he wanted someone to celebrate with afterwards. No matter what it was he was looking for, I'd drive him to Timbuktu if I had to.

We hopped into my dad's car and drove over to Anna's house. I didn't realize how much I appreciated modern cars – power steering, power brakes, power everything, and of course seat belts – until I drove a car in the 1940s. Man, it was a workout just to drive somewhere. No wonder they used cars a lot less, and no wonder we're fat.

The driveway appeared to take us to another county, but at least there was not much snow to contend with. I avoided the ruts as best I could, but it was still a bumpy ride. He didn't want to call ahead of time and ruin the surprise, so we hoped she would be there.

I had never seen Bill so nervous. Normally, he just lets things drip right off him like he wore some kind of oily repellent. But not now. He fidgeted with his fingers the whole way over, twisting his thumbs together like he was wrestling himself. In a couple ways, he actually was.

"You think she'll like it?" he asked. "It took me forever to pick it out. Nice people at the store and all, but they all start to look alike after a while. The rings, that is, not the people..."

The ring. The familiar thin, gold ring with the small diamond solitaire. I looked at it in his hand like it was a familiar friend I hadn't seen in a while. It was like he had run over to my house and snagged it right out of the box.

"She'll love it!" I said with as much gusto as I could muster.

We arrived at the house, and I parked the car at a circular end of the driveway. The house stood to our right, and a small barn nestled behind a large maple lay straight ahead. Beyond that was a wide open field bordered by a row of trees way down by the river. I couldn't see them, but I knew they were there.

I waited and watched him out of the corner of my eye. He continued sitting there without moving a muscle. The fidgeting had stopped but it soon became a problem of momentum, or lack thereof.

"Bill? Well... are you going?" I also wanted to make sure he was still alive.

He angled his head then gazed in my direction. "Oh yeah. Yup, I'm ready."

He continued looking ahead out the front window even though there were no posted signs with answers on them. It was an expression of being either deep in thought or deep in prayer, shrouded within an unperceived difference.

His upper body shuddered like he had become possessed with a spirit of decisiveness. Whatever it was he quickly sprang into action.

"Well, here goes nothing..." he said.

He opened the car door and gave me one last, hopeful glance. He beamed and winked with his newfound confidence. Then he turned around and headed toward the house.

"Good luck, Bill," I yelled out as he was walking away. I shut the door behind him.

He held up his left hand to acknowledge me, holding out his index finger and thumb to resemble a pistol pointing toward the sky.

He waltzed up to the front porch with a newfound spring in his step. His head was raised, and he even did a slight jump off the last step landing on both feet simultaneously. The car filled quickly with my amusement.

The sparkle of the engagement ring was subdued only by the darkness of his pants pocket, and he fidgeted with it as he rang the doorbell awaiting a reply. He traded off kicking his feet back on their heels, shifting side to side as he waited. I tried to follow his rhythm but couldn't guess what song was in his head.

The door soon opened and Anna answered. She gave him a quick hug and offered for him to come inside. As Bill disappeared into the depths of the house, she grabbed the door firmly with her right hand. As she was about to close it behind him, she noticed me sitting in the car. Her timid wave was the last thing I saw before she shut the door.

She was always a difficult one to read, but I swore she looked as if she was about to do something she had planned and anticipated for a while.

I slid forward in the driver's seat and slanted my head back on the headrest. With my arms folded around my chest, my eyes closed out of reflex. As I focused on the soothing hum of the engine running, I drifted off quicker than I expected. I felt like a modern day disciple whose master had just left to pray in a garden. I knew I couldn't stay awake. That was asking too much of me.

A thick fog blanketed the open field, as if the recent temperature fluctuations wanted me second-guessing on depth and direction. The unseen noises that came from the nearby field startled me. It was the recognizable sound of laughter and play, with both kids and adult voices in the mix.

My interest was piqued so I decided to check it out. I slipped out of the car and headed toward the foggy pasture. I couldn't see more than ten feet in front of me, so finding my way across the vast field was difficult.

As I got closer, I could pick out what looked like an entire family playing catch in the open field. The playground ball was bright red, acting like a lighthouse as I maneuvered across the unknown. I gained confidence in my step as I focused on the shiny ball bouncing randomly back and forth. I got close enough to where I could almost reach out and touch them, yet they appeared to be floating inside a hovering cloud.

"Hey, that looks like fun!" I proclaimed, but to no acknowledgement.

They formed a small circle to play catch but not tightly enough to enclose the laughter of the two kids. The boy looked taller and noticeably older than the young girl. A middle-aged lady joined them whom I suspected was their mother, and next to her was an older couple joining in the fun. I approached the older couple who were both right in front me.

"Excuse me," I said. "Why are you out here playing catch? This fog is pretty darn thick." No response.

I leaned forward and tapped the older man on the shoulder. He appeared startled as he turned around quickly and looked me right in the eye. I instantly recognized his crew cut and the starched white shirt.

"Ha!" I bellowed impulsively with a deep, guttural voice. The loud sound forced the older lady to quickly rotate her shoulder to the left and peer right at me. Without thinking, I breathed in deeply and sucked in an abundance of heavy, damp air.

It should not have surprised me as much as it did, but it was clear Anna was looking as pretty as ever. But it did. She was supposed to be someone else.

* * *

The knock on the passenger door startled me. My hands popped off my chest and flailed in the air in front of me. My head bounced off the backrest, and my left hand firmly hit the steering wheel.

"Ow!" I violently shook my hand hoping the pain would subside.

I rubbed my eyes. Of course, someone would be watching, but I was happy to see it was Bill standing right by the door. Somehow the doors had locked, so I reached over to open it for him.

"Well, how'd it go, Bill?"

The look on his face said it all as he fell into the passenger seat. The door slammed as he slouched down to wrap his head with his right arm leaning against the window. His heavy breathing quickly fogged up the window.

"Just leave!" he said in a muffled yell. I watched him closely, startled yet focused, then realized he meant it as much as it sounded.

I drove off as fast as I could, snow splashing outward like the parting of a salty sea. I drove past our homes, past the businesses on Main Street, and headed for Timbuktu. The further the better.

But I instinctively veered toward our fishing lake outside of town. I figured there was always peace in what we knew.

When we arrived, I made a U-turn onto the muddy shoulder. We stopped abruptly, causing loose gravel to hurtle in all directions. His window was completely fogged up, and his head still enveloped in his arm. He barely moved since he had returned to the car.

I also sat motionless, wondering how much time I should give him to gather his thoughts. Where did his thoughts go such that they needed to be gathered? I didn't know, but I also couldn't help but ask the inevitable.

"So... what happened?"

He reached for the door handle and jumped out of the car. I followed him as he fell into the sandy dirt encircling the lake. He exhaled a deep sigh right when I plopped down next to him. His slouched shoulders looked like he was carrying a heavy knapsack on his back.

We sat for a while just watching and listening to the sights and sounds of the water. The hearty birds that hung around for the winter swam around the marsh in seemingly effortless fashion. But I knew better. I knew how they furiously paddled with their feet, albeit all underwater and out of view.

"She said she didn't want to be married to a dead soldier," he finally said.

"What the hell does that mean?"

"It means what you think it means! What a bum rap. That broad..."

A gaggle of Canadian geese flew overhead, eventually landing softly onto the cold, peaceful water. Their wings spread as they eased onto the frigid lake. Only a few small ripples formed after their impressive landing. It was a calming sight to see. Unfortunately, I was the only one who did.

"She had the nerve to tell me I wasn't going to be there for her," he mumbled then jerked his body to one side like the wrestling match with himself was not complete. "I don't have a choice. I'm going off to fight a goddamn war!"

I felt the harshness of that statement just as much as him, if not more. It encompassed so much for me: the separation from my family to the loneliness of being in an unfamiliar world. It was forever since I last saw my mom and sister. It had gotten to the point where I didn't think about them very much. Not because I didn't care, but precisely because I did.

And yes, the war. The goddamn war. That's where I knew he would spend the next five years of his life, not out of choice but purely out of necessity and obligation. Unfortunately, for a story-loving man like my grandfather, it would be an unproductive time period where so much would happen but very little would come out of it. At least, anything he would want to tell.

Not to be selfish, but would I have to go with him? I was 18, in excellent shape, and as draftable as anybody. I had already put my first life on hold. Would I have to do it to my second? Would I even be able to keep that life, no matter where or when it was? As I looked out over the placid lake, my view suddenly became tainted by a jumbled blend of empathy, fear, and anger.

Don't get me wrong, the whole trip back was in many ways a wonderful experience. But it was supposed to be about getting closer to my grandpa, wasn't it? The baseball, the fishing, and spending time with the family – especially the dad – I never had. I learned my lessons. Wasn't I done yet? I just didn't understand how going off to war fit into this new life that had been constructed. Somebody else clearly chose it for me. Not only did it not fit into my idyllic picture of heaven, but it wasn't part of my idealized earth either.

Who's controlling this damn universe? I wanted my life back, and I would have paid anything to buy my ticket back to the life I knew and had grown to love. Somebody stop this godforsaken roller coaster. I wanted off!

There was no way I desired to go fight in some bloody war. Unfortunately, I didn't have a say in the matter. Neither did Bill.

"That's a terrible thing for her to say," I exclaimed. "What can you do? You're going to serve your damn country!"

"I have no idea, John, no idea. We have to go, don't we? I mean, we don't have a choice. There's nothing I can do."

This was the one time I hated the word 'we'.

I picked up a stick and started drawing circles in the mushy dirt. As I drew, I concentrated on the heavy beating of my heart. I heard him alright, but I didn't have an answer. Honestly, looking back on it now, I'm not really sure there was one.

Time has this funny way of passing by at various speeds. Unfortunately, I didn't get to choose the speed either. I'm still not sure how long we sat there, serenaded by the calmness of the tranquil water. It was a gentle reminder which I sorely needed at that moment.

"Remember our fishing trip here, Bill? I'm guessing the eaglets are all grown up by now."

I held my hand up to my eyes hoping it would help me locate the nest across the small lake. At least from my vantage point, it was nowhere to be found.

"Yeah, I do," he answered softly. "They're flying on their own without a care in the world."

Bill stood up and searched for rocks in the dirt. He cupped his hand to hold the few he had found nearby. He tossed the first one, then a second, and a third. As they skipped on the lake, small ripples spread across the water like the sound waves of a slow-motion yell.

He grabbed the ring out of his pocket and twirled it in his fingers. He stopped to get a good look at it, then glanced back and forth between the water and the ring. I knew what he was thinking.

"I think you should keep it, Bill," I whispered.

I watched him rub the tears from his face with his muddy hands. He was far from caring what he looked like. The streaks of dirt on his white shirt made him look weary and beaten. I felt awful noticing. He dropped the last rock he was holding, and it landed right by my feet. It was too bad. It was a perfect skipping stone. Flat and round like a silvery coin snatched out of a wishing well.

"Why the hell do you say that?" he asked.

"Well, we all need reminders of our sacrifices," I hesitated not really certain myself where I was going with it. "You know, the unplanned things that throw our lives for a loop. Think how boring life would be if everything always went as planned."

He laughed, "I'd take boring right now, actually."

I stood up right next to him. My hands drifted to where they needed to be, and his shoulder was warm to the touch. We watched the birds over the water for quite a while before either of us moved.

He eventually placed the shiny ring back into the darkness of his pocket.

He glanced down and spotted the rock he had recently dropped. It was easy to pick out as both its affinity and perfection were unmistakable. As he picked it up, he realized instantly how good it was. Certainly, it was amongst a sea of stones and any of them might have worked, but this one was perfect for him. He was familiar with it, but apparently he needed to drop it then find it again to appreciate it.

For some reason, I instantly thought of Arlis. I realized then that I had fallen in love with her, but in an unexplained, different sort of way. Her distinctive mannerisms, her warm face, her soft, gentle hand. I also realized that for the first time in my life, I was leading Bill and that he would follow.

Without hesitation, he leaned to his right and threw the rock with the best sidearm toss I've ever seen. It initially landed on the thin ice, but then eventually found the open water. We didn't even try to count the number of times it skipped. We didn't have to.

It's funny how my memory has changed over the years, but I swear to this day that rock skipped all the way across the lake. The large oak tree hanging out over the marsh awaited its arrival.

It was a long distance to travel between the thin ice and the large oak. Trust me, I speak from experience. I can't say for certain, but if the eagle was still there, he watched the whole thing.

Chapter 17

After a day that lasted much longer than I expected, Bill and I finally headed for home. I turned my lights on as we entered town, trying to direct the car through the fine mist that started falling out of the blotchy, grey sky.

"It's certainly been an interesting day to say the least." I didn't know what else to say. I parked the car in front of Bill's house, my hands firmly gripping the steering wheel.

He gazed in my direction but never made eye contact. "Yeah, I guess I'll get over it... eventually. I just hope I can find someone else willing to put up with me."

He let out a short, uncomfortable laugh. The more I thought about his comment, the more I thought how funny and ironic it was. "Trust me, Bill, you will. I promise."

"Thanks for the encouragement, John." He glanced toward me with a long, drawn face, looking like a caricature of himself. "I appreciate you being there for me today. I'll be sure to return the favor someday."

"I'm sure you will, Bill, I'm sure you will."

"Well, we'll see you later old pal." He paused as if grasping for a thought. "You know… maybe we could try and get a pickup game going tomorrow. Might be our last one for a long time."

I knew he would come back. He returned to what he knew, important after being beaten by life. I glanced at him, realizing in a way we were in the same predicament. We also coincidentally found the same solution. Funny how that works. It had been a long journey since the game by the mill. One winding yet circular path.

"I would love that, Bill. I really would."

He finally opened the door and ran up his steps as the rain started to come down harder. I've always loved the musty smell of rain, and this time was no different.

He hesitated when he got to the porch and turned around to wave. It was a surprisingly hearty and reassuring wave. He became an easy one for me to read, and I was certain of what he was about to do.

I headed home and parked the trusty car in the garage. They certainly didn't have all the conveniences of modern automobiles, but I sure grew even fonder of those old cars. Built to last forever.

I ran into the house and tugged on my shirt a few times in the foyer to dry off. The dampness had soaked through to my skin. I almost ran upstairs to change, but I took a quick sniff. The aroma in the house reminded me it was time for dinner, so I dashed into the kitchen and sat down at the table, right next to my dad.

He looked at me as soon I grabbed the chair, "That rain is really coming down. I hope you didn't get caught in it, John."

It bugged me in a way. Didn't he have more important things to talk about besides the weather? Wasn't his son about to head off to war? The nuances of the present apparently obstructed his perspective of the future, and it annoyed the hell out of me. I loved the man, but I thought right there he was losing whatever sanity he had.

"Not really," I answered. "It only started falling after we got home."

"Where'd you go?" my mom asked.

"Bill and I were just out and about, that's all. A very eventful day, no doubt about that."

It was a small town. I figured they would find out eventually.

They both sat there leaning into the table and clearly expecting me to fill in the details. They both stopped their eating, my father with fork in midair. What did they want me to say, that my best friend had just gotten his heart split in two?

My heart was shattered for him, even though I didn't really care for Anna in the first place. But I knew he would recover eventually and all would be well. However, I wasn't sure when I would. My bad day was making me cynical, and right then I wished my parents would stop staring at me.

They were both shrouded with disappointment as they could clearly tell no details were forthcoming. They glanced down at their plates then reluctantly kept eating. I joined them even though I was not hungry in any way.

The conversation inevitably shifted to other topics, from the weather to church to Christmas, or any combination thereof. I mostly listened and ate intermittently.

"So... are you helping set up the Christmas decorations at church, honey?" my dad asked. "That's right around the corner."

"Yes, I am tomorrow night, actually," she answered. "The tree was cut today out by the Blakeley's farm, so we'll set it up by the altar then decorate it. Gladys is in charge of the bazaar this year, so let me know if there is anything you'd like to sell. It's a wonderful fundraiser."

I sat silently and motionless. My food and spirits getting colder by the minute. I couldn't understand why these people were making such a sorry attempt at normalcy. Were they completely insensible to what was going on around them? Did they not know so many of their friends' sons would soon die?

"I've got something to sell," I piped in.

Both of them shot me peculiar looks, as if they were shocked to learn I could speak. I also didn't own very much, at least any disposable items that were worth selling. But I knew better.

"Oh... that's great, John." My mom spoke with an annoying slowness. "Whenever you get a chance, just bring it down. I can take it over to church anytime."

"I'll get it now, actually." I jumped out of my chair and hurried upstairs. My heels struck hard on the stairs reminding my parents where I was and where I was going.

I entered my room and glanced around. It was fairly empty, especially by today's excessive standards. A small, wooden nightstand sat next to my bed which was covered neatly in an off-white blanket. The few pictures on the wall were from places I didn't know nor care about.

The simple oak dresser stood innocently over by the closet, leaning against the light brown trim. To me, it looked weighted down by the contents on top like it was trying to tell me to get rid of them. The box perched on top, sheepishly trying to hide behind the trophies. But I knew it was there. I knew they were all there.

I sat down on the end of my bed, feeling guilty I had messed up the neatly folded covers. I stared intently at the dresser and considered my options. The trophies boldly stood at attention. Shiny, new, and in obvious recognition of past accomplishments. But they were not what I focused on.

The box became much more rustic and tattered in the last few months. It was not aging gracefully, and it was looking weathered beyond its years. I had no idea why. But outward appearance was only part of the problem. Its contents slowly vanished before my eyes, and I was unsure how to replace them.

I quickly unlatched the box and glanced inside. The ring was gone. The box accelerated its emptiness with each passing day, a process I only then figured out even existed.

Certainly, there could be other places to store the remaining items. There were only three, and they were all so small. Even the feather, which signified a great memory, wasn't worth my attention. I figured they would all dematerialize at some point, anyway.

Maybe my bad day clouded my thinking. I questioned why my grandpa even gave me the worn-out, rustic chest in the first place. Was it not to store various mementos from his life? Then why did they disappear after every momentous event? Dammit, I wanted that muddy ball, that toothpick, that ring. I wanted to cherish them forever, and I was furious I was not being given that chance.

It just didn't feel like I needed that box anymore. It would just be extra baggage as I headed off to fight in a stupid war that to me was already over and done with. The history books have already told me how it ends. Why did we need to fight it again? I wasn't even sure if I'd come back, let alone require a silly little box to remind me of everything and everyone that had left me in my life. I wanted no part in the affair.

Maybe it was the war that clouded my thinking. The thought of heading off to a faraway land – an unrecognizable place where absolutely everything would be new – infuriated me. A place forced upon me that would steal the life I knew and replace it with something totally different. A place never-ending in time, forcing my heart to bleed for whom I had left, not knowing if I would ever return. A place where things and actions and places would become more important than the people around me.

Then it hit me. I was already at that place.

I dropped my head in my hands and wept harder than I ever had in my life.

* * *

I wiped my eyes on my sleeves and attempted to look as normal as possible. But the mirror didn't help the cause, reflecting my blood-red eyes and blotchy skin. I abhor when others know I have cried. The questions, the pity. I grabbed what I needed and ran downstairs. I juggled what I was holding as they shifted when I walked. My feet pounded on the stairs.

When I stepped into the kitchen, I instantly focused on their reactions. They each took their last bite of dinner, then glanced up at their incoming son. My dad slowly stretched his neck to the side, looking like a turtle coming out of his shell.

"You sure you want to get rid of that?" my mom asked. "Seemed like only yesterday that meant a lot to you."

I glanced down at my arms and was certain of what I was getting rid of. I didn't want them anymore. "Yeah, I'm sure. What would I do with some old trophies anyway? They just collect dust on my dresser."

They looked quizzically at each other then back at me.

"Well… if you really want to get rid of those. Ok then," my dad said as he scratched his chin. He had clearly forgotten to shave that day, the first day I had ever seen him with stubble. Must have had other stuff on his mind.

"Yeah, I do. I just... I just realized I have more important things in my life."

Those trophies weren't really mine anyway, but I'm guessing my counterpart wouldn't have argued my decision. I was about to take his place in a role I never signed up for, so I got the short stick as it was.

Besides, they were reminders of innocent days of youth that had long since passed.

Chapter 18

Our snow-covered lawn looked so beautiful in the morning, almost as if a blanket had been laid, covering everything that used to be there. It looked so new, so fresh, so different. I was stunned how quiet our humble house could be, especially when I woke up before everyone else. That included my father.

I made some coffee using our stove top percolator – surprised myself I figured out how to do it – and grabbed the morning newspaper that had just arrived on our front steps. I was impressed how the paperboy had somehow delivered it without getting it wet.

The news wasn't all bad, but it wasn't all good either. I skipped the first few pages as I already knew the inevitable. They had just announced the reporting procedure for the draft, and I should be expecting my draft notice any day now. The war was now a runaway train headed down a one-way track. Nobody knew where it was going. Except for me, of course.

Even though the weather had taken a turn for the worse, we felt we needed to play a pickup game. One last time. We didn't know how many opportunities we would have to do what we wanted. Bill had declared he wanted to play baseball again, and I was not about to let some stupid snow get in the way of playing ball with my grandpa. He mentioned he was going to round up the other boys and meet us at Riverside by 10 a.m. That gave me plenty of time to catch up on the news and warm up by the fireplace.

"Well, you're up early," my dad remarked, startling me as I hadn't heard him come in the living room. The paper shook ever so slightly masked entirely by the crackling fireplace.

"Yup, just catching up on what's going on." My eyes shifted between him and the newspaper.

"Not a lot of good news, is there? Where do you think this war is headed, John?"

"Not sure." The pain of knowing but not telling was almost unbearable.

He walked over and sat down in the other chair opposite the radio. His slippers glided along the wooden floor, sounding like coarse sandpaper. The newly-risen sun peeked through the shades, giving a newfound intensity to the room. The reflective blanket of snow on the ground made me wonder if the actual source of light was from above or from below.

"You know, Dad, I'm not worried about the war," I confided. "I'm ready to go wherever I'm needed. Being in a foreign land doesn't scare me at all."

I decided to skip the chit-chat and go right to what we really needed to talk about. He shifted unsteadily in his chair. I already knew I was alone in that sentiment. I just didn't know how much.

"Well, your mother's really worried about you, John. She doesn't want you to go anywhere."

"She doesn't have a choice." I shrugged my shoulders.

"That's true, John. She doesn't."

"Then… she shouldn't worry about me if she doesn't have a choice."

"Well, I guess that comes with being a parent, John. She just… she doesn't want to lose her only child."

I was not expecting that at all. I watched him for longer than normal, making sure I heard him correctly. But he was right, which was not to say I was wrong. Sometimes I search for things only to find they're sitting right in front of me all along. The most obvious things can be the most elusive. The fact that I was their only child had completely escaped me. In more ways than one, I always thought of my sister, Sarah, in my old life back home. Man, how I missed her.

I originally believed I had been thrown into my ideal life in 1941. It included a father and wonderful times spent with my grandpa. However, in a couple of ways, I questioned if that was really the case. More specifically, I was beginning to believe the opposite was true.

"I hope you feel the same way, Dad. I hope it's not just a Mom thing."

He looked at me in a timeless infinity but never said a word. He didn't have to. I saw a reflection of myself in the moistness of his eyes, and I instantly knew what I meant to him. The silent room echoed the unyielding sentiment. It was what I needed to know.

* * *

I threw on some long underwear and a warm cap, added my baseball gear, then headed over to Bill's place. The air felt cold, but there wasn't a cloud in the sky. While the grass was still covered in snow, the warm morning sun did its best to melt what was unlucky enough to fall on the sidewalk. But there were still remnants. My metal cleats provided good traction on the shaded areas that had iced over during the evening.

"Hey Bill!" I shouted as I approached his house. He had been sitting on the porch even though I was five minutes early. He held a cup of hot chocolate in one hand and his glove in the other. He dropped the glove on his lap as I arrived.

"Beautiful mornin', John," he said.

"Like an old friend, eh?" I nodded toward his glove as I walked up the front steps.

He looked down, "Oh, this old thing? Yeah, it hasn't changed a bit since I last saw it."

"But you certainly have."

He glanced up at me and made a weak attempt at a smile. He jumped to his feet, grabbed his bat and glove, and then followed me as we headed over to Riverside Park. Our old stomping ground that felt further away than it used to.

It was a quiet morning in town as only a few cars were out and about. We considered driving over there, but I was always a fan of walking on new-fallen snow. Felt like walking on a crunchy cloud. However, this would be the first time I would ever do it to go play baseball.

I wish I would have taken a picture of the river that morning. With snow-covered banks and steam rising from its center, the river steadily flowed wherever it wanted to go. If only I had my cell phone with me to take a picture. I chuckled to myself but soon realized I didn't need it. To this day, I can still describe exactly what that river looked like.

Bill and I were the first ones there, so we threw our bags in the dugout and got ready. Bill tightened his laces while I searched for my glove. I remembered the first time my bag was in that dugout. I had just arrived, in more ways than one.

I looked around and noticed the place hadn't changed a bit. The same shiny metal bench where I nursed my head. The same puddle of muddy water that collected near the entrance, where the guys splattered me with their gloves. And the same chain link fence that provided a categorized view of his story come to life.

The crunch of the snow under our cleats provided the only other sounds besides the river's flow off in the distance. We headed out to play catch.

"Hey, Eddy! Nice of you to make it," I yelled as he approached, glove and bat in hand.

"I think baseball should be a winter sport, boys. This is great out here," he declared. "Imagine DiMaggio sliding across the snow to catch one in center. That'd be tops, man."

"Eddy, you can't even catch in good weather," Bill quipped. "How do you expect to catch any better in snow?"

"I can definitely catch one of your weak pop-ups, there, chrome-dome."

Bill chucked the ball at Eddy, barely missing his head. He was saved by a slight duck of his shoulders. The two of them continued yapping away like they were long lost brothers. A language all their own. They were really going to miss each other during the war.

Harry was the next to show up. He played catch with Eddy right about when Charlie arrived. An unfamiliar car also pulled into the parking lot, purposely driving in fast enough to spin out the back wheels. Looked exactly like something Caleb would do. Before I knew it, we were getting close to having enough for a full-fledged game.

"What kinda car is that?" I asked Bill as I threw him the ball. I had gotten used to the vehicles from the 1940s, but I wasn't able to recognize all the makes and models. Honestly, they all started to look the same to me, but I guess that was a trick unfamiliarity played on me.

"Hmm, looks like one of those new Plymouth coupes," he surmised.

"Oh yeah. I had forgotten they came out with that."

It was a burgundy beast with a sloped front grill that looked like watchful eyes plastered onto a rounded face. It only had two doors, yet somehow managed to contain three guys in the back. As they crawled out, I thought they looked familiar but couldn't place from where.

"Hey Bill, who are those clowns?"

He turned his head sharply to get a good view. He threw me the ball then started chuckling, sounding like he knew something no one else did. "You don't recognize 'em, Johnny boy?"

They wore standard white baseball pants, but the scarlet lettering on their caps gave it away. I quickly figured it out then joined him in laughing, almost in unison. The other guys glanced over at us, wondering where our sanity had been lost.

"Who in the world are they, John?" questioned Eddy standing next to me. His gloved hand leaned against his angled hips as he squinted toward the sparse parking lot.

"Looks like half the Hartland team," I told him. "I'm guessing they've come to join us. Gee, I wonder who invited 'em…"

It was the entire infield plus their star pitcher, and apparently Bill had kept in touch with them in the last few months. Didn't surprise me. As I tossed the ball to Bill, he winked at me as if to say, 'this is gonna be fun.'

They had five players and we had nine, so Charlie and Hank played outfield for their team to make it seven on seven. We took the field first, so they warmed up to bat. The infield sure was sloppy from the recent rain and snow, but not nearly as bad as that muddy game back in April. The layer of permafrost below made the dirt harder than it looked. There was still snow covering the entire outfield grass, but it was melting fast.

As Bill and I trotted out to the field together, I watched his excitement but sensed his anxiety. He clearly wanted to do this, but he had other things on his mind. I knew what he was thinking.

"You ready for this, bud?" I asked him.

He exhaled in a loud, deep manner, making me wonder if more than air left him. He tilted his head skyward then looked at me with a confident gaze.

"Yup... let's do it!"

I jogged over to the pitcher's mound and picked up the ball. It was cold and muddy, but it felt good in my hands. The harsh seams and soft leather provided a contrast I never noticed before. It had been a while, but I figured it was like riding a bike. Bill headed out to center but stopped abruptly at second. He quickly turned around and trotted back to the mound. I watched him the round trip.

He snatched the ball out of my hand. "Mind if I pitch?"

"Sure... I guess so," was the only thing I could think to say. I was shocked. It was the first time he had ever offered to pitch in a game.

I stepped off the mound, wiped my hand on my pants, then folded my arms to watch.

He owned the mound like it was a familiar stomping ground. One, ten, a hundred times before. He caressed the dirt with his cleats and smoothed out the surface to his liking. He danced and scuffled on the rubber to loosen the mud, then kicked it away in a flurry. It was now his.

With upright shoulders and a pumped out chest, he faced the catcher, his hands meeting inside his glove. He paused, building momentum. Suddenly, in one swift motion, his body curled into a powerful windup, his arm flew back as he stretched forward, landed hard, and heaved his first pitch.

It missed by a mile.

The ball careened off the backstop and eventually came to rest near the visitor dugout. The catcher ran over and threw it back, while their first batter waiting in the on-deck circle shot Bill a perplexed look.

Don't get me wrong, he wasn't all bad. Every now and then he got lucky enough that the ball flew over the plate. But the one thing he had on his side was nobody knew where the ball was going, not him and especially not the batters.

It certainly set the stage for an eventful game of baseball.

They scored in the top of the first on a routine fly ball I should have caught out in center. But nothing is routine when playing in snow. Charlie and Hank contributed to their offense with back-to-back doubles in the third. They appeared to be having a blast, even if they played for the wrong team.

Bill and I made certain we took the lead in the bottom of the third. As I stepped into the batter's box, I peered over the pitcher's shoulder and watched Bill take his lead off second. I knew right then and there I would do whatever it took to bring him home. First pitch, I slashed a double down the third base line. It died in the snow, but at least it went far enough out for Bill to beat the throw home from his good, old friend, the third baseman. The guy was still shivering, and this time I hoped for his sake it was from the cold.

In the top of the fourth with us up 3-2, Bill did something I never expected. With two outs and bases loaded, he stepped back off the mound with a surprised uncertainty. The first baseman from Hartland was up to bat, a massive lumberjack of a man who looked mysteriously like the Brawny paper towel guy. For all I knew, he was.

I almost called time to run in and chat with Bill. He glanced down at the damp ball in his glove, then looked at me out in center. I couldn't see that far in, but somehow I knew he was smiling at me. He quickly hopped back on the mound and adjusted the ball in his glove longer than usual. He set from the stretch, then glared at the batter for what felt like eternity. The bat swayed back and forth, impatiently waiting for the critical pitch. We all held our breath. Silence overwhelmed.

And there it came.

As soon as the ball propelled out of Bill's hand, I instantly recognized what he had thrown. I knew it well. His motion was more of a shot putter than a pitcher, typical of someone who doesn't throw the pitch very often. But it fluttered to the plate like a frigid butterfly. I'm not sure I could have thrown the knuckleball any better.

Mr. Brawny waited patiently for the unhurried pitch. His hefty weight shifted to his back foot, leaning firm against his muscular leg. When the ball finally arrived, he unleashed a mighty swing for the fence. The ball plummeted at the front edge of the plate, heading straight for the muddy ground. But he was an experienced hitter. He adjusted his arms mid-swing then abruptly made contact. The baseball blasted off the end of the bat like a golf ball off the head of a precision driver.

It was a good thing there was not a cloud in the sky, or else the mile-high pop up would have ignited a nasty snowstorm. I normally don't play outfield, so I had trouble following the flight of the ball. I drifted in but started losing it in the bright midday sun. I was bound and determined to catch that stupid ball. As it dropped out of the vast sea of blue, I sensed I had sorely misjudged its distance. I ran in as fast as I could in the sloppy, melting snow.

"I got it! I got it!" I yelled at the top of my lungs. Harry was running out from short but backed off when he heard me yell.

My cleats held firm with every step as I barreled in from center.

It was the first time I had ever slid in snow during a baseball game. I stretched out my glove then hit the snow right as the ball finally returned to Earth. I heard the ball hit my glove, but all I remember was sliding until the infield dirt was in reach.

When I came to a rest, I surprisingly felt something in my glove so I lifted it in the air. Somehow, I had managed to catch that darn thing. I quickly hopped up then flipped the ball to Harry as I ran in. He shook his head in disbelief and began running toward the dugout with me.

"Nice catch!" Bill acknowledged when we reached the mound. "I could have done without all the drama, though."

"Dontcha see? I had to make it dramatic," I confessed, "just so you'd appreciate it."

Not surprisingly, the entire front of my pants and jersey were dirty, wet, and cold. But it was all worth it. Even the Hartland guys gave me high fives at my miraculous catch. We all hovered near home, wondering what to do next. It was, after all, a good place to be.

"Let's call that game, boys," Bill announced. "I'm freezing my butt off."

"Sounds good to me. We'd better head home anyway," replied one of the Hartland guys.

"That was a blast! Thanks for coming, boys," Bill added as he shook all of their hands, "Forgive me for the game back in April?"

The first baseman grabbed his hand and yanked Bill toward him. He dropped his shoulder pretending to tackle Bill, taking him by surprise. Bill literally bounced off the guy like he had collided with a thick, pronounced wall.

"Sure, why not?" he bellowed. The guy had a deep, thunderous voice like he was calling his blue ox, Babe.

It was odd seeing Bill so uncomfortable, but I'm guessing he really wanted to seal up some old wounds that day. Can't say I blame him.

* * *

It was an amazing day for a game of baseball. Not perfect by any means, but then it wouldn't have been so memorable if it was. However, I made a pact with myself to never play baseball again on a snow-covered field. It was just too unique, too much fun to ever attempt to recreate. Some things are only worth doing once. Not because they aren't special, but exactly because they are.

There were no clues that this entire group of men was about to head off to fight a bloody war in a faraway, unfamiliar place. Some would see frontline fighting, where bullets and mortars would haphazardly fly to and fro in a deadly game of chess. A game that somebody else understood, that somebody else controlled. Some would come home to parades and honored fanfare, while some would never make it home.

But nary a word was spoken about that uncertain future. We were having too much fun, lost in the moment of playing a game we all loved so dearly. Differences were put aside and the game was played the way it was meant to be played.

It was enjoyable, and it was entertaining. The game provided that rare opportunity to escape to somewhere we really wanted to be but couldn't stay.

Dare I say, we were carefree.

Chapter 19

Everyone in town noticed the Selective Service office that opened in January on East Main Street. Local Board #165 was housed in an old brick building where the old Post Office used to be, right next to the hardware store. 'Buy a hammer, join the war effort… all in one trip!' Or so the joke went.

The only hint of what it had become was the makeshift 'Selective Service' sign printed neatly on a large, off-white sheet of paper. It was taped to the front window just to the right of the doorway. The place had an unmistakable temporary feel to it, like a traveling salesman who would pick up his wares and unexpectedly escape into the darkness of the night. Of course, those types of salesmen weren't salesmen at all. They were thieves.

Bill and I received our draft notices in the mail on the same day. Small, brown postcards, stamped with the address of the local board. At the time, I found it ironic. How many people can honestly say they were drafted on the same day as their grandpa?

We were both now officially 1-A, or available for unrestricted military service. We were told to report to the Selective Service office within the week.

Bill dropped by our house to show me his newfound mail. He dashed in with a spring in his step like a little kid who had just received a birthday gift. Personally, I thought he was a bit wacko.

"You ready for this, John?" He held out his prized, one-of-a-kind draft card that happened to look a lot like mine.

"Yeah, I'm really excited…" I looked upon my card with a disdain I typically reserved for my drill-obsessed dentist. It was difficult to get excited about going to war, especially for a pessimistic cynic like me. Quite the opposite. I hated it.

Somehow, I knew all the questions to ask, yet none of the answers. Where would I be shipped off to amongst the European or Pacific theaters? What kind of role would I play? Worst of all: would I even be able to come home? The thought of it all was making me nauseous.

Like many other men between the ages of 18 to 45, I had not signed up to do this. I could have registered as a conscientious objector, although time travel would have been a lousy excuse not to fight. But that's the nature of conscription during a time of war. Nobody is immune to the process.

"I guess it was expected they'd lower the minimum age to 18," Bill pointed out. "I mean, we can fight just as well as anybody twice our age. Even better I'd say."

Great. My age had allowed me to drink, and now it allowed me to go off to war. Like being handed a season pass to a theme park, only to discover the park no longer existed.

I invited Bill in, and we sat down at the kitchen table to chat. As we did, I watched my mom conveniently walk out the back door, most likely to shop downtown. It's not that she didn't like Bill. On the contrary. My parents had no interest whatsoever to discuss the draft or the war. Ever. In fact, they purposely avoided the topic.

"You're right about that," I responded. "I have no doubt we can contribute to the war."

"Contribute? Hell, I'm doin' more than contribute. I'm fightin' to the death."

I fidgeted with the pencil that was sitting on the table, realizing quickly he was much more ready than I was. I told myself and my parents I was ready. But push had come to shove. The differences in my attitude with Bill's seemed to be a generational thing, but then again, we were the same age.

"You know what, let's just register right now," Bill proposed. "What are we waitin' for?"

"Well… I'm as ready as I'll ever be," which wasn't very far from the truth.

We headed over to the local draft board. It was early on a Saturday morning, but surprisingly there was only a short wait. I didn't recognize any of the men in line ahead of us. They were in their 20s and 30s, wore black felt Fedoras, dark suits and long trench coats. They looked like gangsters working for Al Capone, so I was happy they were signing up to fight on our side. Compared to them, Bill and I were sorely underdressed.

I don't think the man at the sign-up table had ever smiled in his life. At least, not in the act of signing up boys to quickly become men or die trying. We first filled out our registration cards and were instructed to remove our shirts and wait in line for the physical. I had still not gotten used to the fact that men in those days were in much better physical condition, even Capone's brutes. Wait until their grandkids introduce them to Twinkies and Ho-Hos.

We walked around the sign-up table and down the hall, then waited in a short line along the outside wall of a large, well-lit room. The dark oak floors and arched entranceway gave it a ceremonial feel, while the makeshift sectionals covered in white sheets felt haphazard and informal.

Bill went first. He stood in perfect posture for the doctor and had his vitals and eyesight checked. I couldn't help but notice the swollen muscles on his arms, his stomach as flat as a smooth rock. I watched his every move, astounded that the skinny, hairless young man standing before me was actually my grandpa. I never got used to that.

His checkup was over before I knew it. They informed him to step down, quickly signed and stamped his card, then handed it back to him.

"Next," the doctor announced.

I walked over and stood as upright as I could, my hands on my side. A cold draft entered the room, and my stomach muscles tightened as the stethoscope touched my bare skin. The doctor was giving me an extra amount of attention, poking and prodding, which both puzzled and annoyed me. I knew I was in excellent health.

"How long have you had that?" He pointed toward my head.

It caught me by surprise as I had completely forgotten about it. The mark had clearly affected my eyesight, but I didn't think I did too poorly on the charts.

"Not long. Nine months. Tops."

The other doctor was called over and briskly inspected my right temple, which was still tender from my baseball injury back in April. When he slowly pushed on it with his thumb, I jumped and yelled. My eyes watered out of reflex. It would have been rude for me to punch him in return, but I strongly considered it. Somehow, the bump had not completely healed, even after nine long months. Nobody said very much about it, including me.

I hated thinking about that game again. But I had to. It was a line drive I should have caught, even if the rain pelted me and the field was muddier than a pigpen. Unacceptable conditions for a baseball game. But I was there, my glove in ready position. I've caught that a hundred times before. It was mine.

I used to think the entire play was a complete and utter failure, but it was far greater than that. To call it a mere failure would be such a simplistic explanation, like calling a funeral a mere ceremony.

While the doctors conferred for what felt like an hour, I impatiently glanced around the room. Bill gave me a squinted look while slightly raising his shoulders as if to say 'What's up?' I shrugged back. I didn't have an answer.

They finally wrote something on my registration card.

"Next," the doctor called out as he pointed me to move forward.

I slowly stepped toward Bill with a puzzled look on my face.

"What was that all about?"

"I have no idea, Bill."

I put my shirt back on quicker than normal, attempting to cover the violation, my vulnerability. I then glanced at my registration card. It was stamped as 4-F.

"What the hell does that mean?" I asked Bill. I glanced at his card and saw a 1-C.

I was furious. My card was different. I had to get to the bottom of it. I ran to the check-in table and slammed down my hand. I ignored the dirty looks from the men in line, whether or not they happened to work for Capone.

"Can you tell me what 4-F means?" I yelled hastily at the stoic jerk at the table.

He slowly glanced at me, then at my card.

"It means you're not acceptable for military service." He shooed me away like I was a lost dog begging for a treat. His nonchalance drove me nuts.

"What? Why?"

His back straightened. He briefly looked me in the eye, tilted his head slightly to the side, then further motioned for me to step away from the table.

I walked in disbelief. What had I done to deserve this? I shot a quick glimpse at Bill and could tell he had heard. He stared at the floor with slouched shoulders like the 50-pound sack had returned. He fully understood the implications. And so did I.

He raised his entire torso, "At least you know you won't be in harm's way. Although… watch out for Anna speeding through town. You never know if she might swerve to hit ya."

"Very funny. That would be you she'd aim for, by the way."

I walked home in a complete daze. We marched down the sidewalk, but I barely noticed the nearby dormant trees, let alone acknowledged them. I don't even remember the route we took. Bill, on the other hand, was downright cheery, even though he was the one going off to war. I didn't get it, and I didn't hide it either.

"Why are you so grumpy about this?" Bill asked. "Seems like a good thing to me."

"It's just… I don't know. I feel kinda guilty. I guess I wanted to join you in going to war. To experience what it's like."

I thrust my hands in my pockets, counting the grooves in the sidewalk. They were beginning to tick by slowly like a dying metronome.

Now that the opportunity had been taken away from me, my attitude about the whole thing completely changed. Even though I said it, I still didn't really want to go. But I sure felt like I needed to.

"Why in heck would you wanna do that?" he questioned my sanity.

"I thought we could endure it together. We'd help each other through it. You know, all for one, one for all. I... I wanted to be there for you, Bill." I wiped my nose on my sleeve, a bit embarrassed.

He shuffled his feet as we progressed along the sidewalk. It was cold outside but not enough to keep people indoors. All ages and shapes and sizes trooping up and down Main Street, everyone looking for someplace to go, someone to see, something to do. For some reason, my mind recalls that moment in black and white and gray. Not a vibrant color to be found.

But I ignored the passersby around us. I didn't know them, and they sure didn't know me. It was utter silence as we walked, both of us pondering our separate futures.

"Why do you need a war to have that?" he asked.

Chapter 20

When I returned home, neither of my parents were there. The house suddenly felt cavernous yet warm. I knew my mom would return from the store soon, so I waited patiently in the kitchen. I pulled up a chair and placed the guilty draft card on the table in front of me. I only glanced at it a few times, deciding if I wanted it to suddenly change or stay exactly the same.

My mom entered tentatively, almost like she was trying to sneak up on me. She was clearly hoping Bill would no longer be there. No more talk about war. But little did she know she did want to hear about it.

"Hey Mom, how was the store?"

"Busy place. Lots of people out and about today. Not sure why. You and Bill have a good morning?" She bustled around the kitchen, putting away the groceries into the cupboards and pantry. She looked every which way, except at me.

"We went to the Selective Service today." I knew it would get her attention, whether she showed it or not.

"That's great, John." She sounded like I just told her I found a dust bunny under my bed. I stood up next to her, and she handed me a few canned goods to put away.

"I'm not going."

She opened the ice box and placed the egg carton and milk jug on the shelf. They looked so large in that small box. I wasn't sure what else we could possibly fit in there.

"Not going where?" There was a distinct sharpness in her tone.

I attempted to hand her my draft card, but she pushed it away. It was most likely the last thing in the world she wanted to look at.

"Mom, take a look." I tried again.

"I'm kind of busy right now, John." She placed her hand on her hip. "Can we talk about this later?" Of course, by later she meant never.

"Mom, listen to me." I grabbed her shoulder. "I'm not going to war. I'm ineligible for the draft thanks to the bad bruise on my temple."

She snatched the card out of my hand and quickly scanned it. Her head shook side to side even though she meant to say 'yes.' Her hands reached up around my neck as she kissed me on the cheek. Neither of us flinched when the cans of Campbell's Chicken Noodle soup hit the ground. It was as if we both expected a culmination to solidify the moment.

The good thing was that there was nothing to clean up. She felt good about that. The cans just rolled to a stop against the counter, waiting to be neatly put away. A little dented and worn, but no harm done.

I admit, I like to see people cry. Makes the moment feel more meaningful. Although, it was quite possibly me, not the moment, that was grasping for meaning.

* * *

I headed over to Bill's place. As I entered his bedroom, it was easy to spot the items neatly spread out on his bed. He sat next to them with one knee bent and the other leg draped over the side of the bed. I realized what he was preparing for. He didn't have to do it just yet, but he was clearly restless about leaving soon.

"Finding a few things to take along?" I leaned against his dresser.

He picked up a few of the items: some baseball cards, his glove, and a few of his favorite books. I watched him closely, trying to interpret what he was thinking about as he prepared for war. I couldn't figure him out, nor do I think he really knew anyway.

As he rummaged through his stuff, it actually occurred to me how much those 1940s baseball cards would be worth today. Ted Williams, Stan Musial, Joe DiMaggio, Pee Wee Reese. All legends in their time and all valued at a mint today. But I didn't care.

I immediately recognized it sitting underneath a couple of other books. I had to lean in to see it. It didn't really stand out except for its familiarity. The unmistakable dark leather cover. But it was much smaller than I imagined it would be from those days. I guess I always envisioned people from a long time ago having these humungous Bibles that just sat in the living room collecting dust. The tomes of time. Yet the book was much more than a pocket-sized version stolen from an unsuspecting Gideon at a run-down motel.

I wondered how it would play into his greater story. Now I understood.

"Yup, just lookin' for a few things to bring," he confessed. "They instructed me to only bring two personal items. How in the world do I choose that?"

I walked over and sat down at the other end of his bed. He looked at me, hoping I had an answer.

"That's tricky. Well... I guess you'd want something you can look at now and then to, I don't know, help you through everything."

"Yeah, you're probably right," he agreed then quickly beamed as he picked up his baseball mitt. "You know, I just heard some of the pros are being drafted, too. Maybe I'll get to meet 'em and play some ball. I'll teach DiMaggio a thing or two about playing center."

I laughed hard enough to put my hand on my stomach. As my back arched, my head tilted upward. I'm not sure why I always do that when I laugh loudly. It's like when I'm asked a deep question. I ponder it by scratching my chin and looking toward the sky. The answer, of course, is not written on the ceiling. But it's only natural to expect all answers, all goodness to come from something above us.

"You will, Bill. You will," I agreed. That was one war story I had heard. He would play ball while stationed in Hawaii. Innocent pickup games with some of the greatest players of his generation. How could I forget that? Pros like DiMaggio, Reese, and many more were indeed drafted, and their Army-Navy games on the island were legendary. Perhaps he did teach Joe a thing or two about center. It was Bill's brush with greatness.

But as he said, I didn't need a war to experience that.

"Well, I gotta run, Bill. My parents wanted to go out to eat tonight, so I'd better head home. I guess... I guess I'll see you on the other side."

He chuckled at my choice of words.

I knew I would see him again, but that moment had a sudden sense of finality to it. I wasn't sure why. I extended my hand to give him a shake. He grabbed it firmly, and I looked deeply into his story-filled eyes.

"See you, friend," he replied.

* * *

I knew the two personal items he would bring with him to war were his baseball mitt and his Bible. They were the two pieces of home that helped him get through those difficult times during the war, when anyone would become overtaken with uncertainty. One item to fall back on, the other to fall forward.

The mitt aptly represented baseball, a sport that took us to new and exciting places, was the source of painful loss, yet also our saving grace.

The Bible also epitomized so much for both of us. It was a source of comfort after our experience on the icy lake, provided assurance to me that Bill would be safe during the war, and little did I know at the time, would offer solace for what was to come. It was good to know the past, present, and future could co-exist so peacefully.

Chapter 21

After a wonderful dinner at the Gasthaus with my parents, we headed home. A sudden cold front swept through the area with a vengeance, and the biting wind across the pitch black evening made it treacherous to be out and about. The car slid a few times on the ice, but my dad righted the ship every time. There were very few cars on the road. Apparently, home was a great place to be.

We shook off the snow and hung up our coats in the front closet. My dad quickly started a fire in the fireplace as I sat nearby trying to stay warm by rubbing my hands together. The crackling of the burning wood serenaded the dancing flame, luring me to watch. My parents shared the sofa, and my dad even dared to take off his shoes and prop his feet on the coffee table. Much to my mom's dismay, of course.

But she was unfazed. She laughed, she smiled. They both appeared so at ease, so peaceful in their unhurried mannerisms and slowed, soft tones as they spoke. I knew what they were thinking with the war and all. It turned out so incredibly right for them, and for me, even before it started. But what did we do to deserve it?

My mom made a cherry crisp dessert before we left for dinner that still warmed in the oven. The scent was hearty and pleasant, and I could already taste it. She served it on small white plates with ribbed edges as I brewed the coffee as strong as I liked it. It was, for the most part, a quiet and uneventful evening. Just like my parents wanted it.

"Any big plans for tomorrow, John?" my mom asked as she sat down holding her dessert plate. She swept her hair back with her hand, then looked at me.

"Not much. I suspect I'll hang out with Bill, but nothing planned." I took a small bite then placed my fork back on the plate. "Actually, seems like our best times have been unplanned."

My dad laughed. "Very true. You can't really plan for fun."

There was a prolonged silence as we all continued eating.

"Or the heartaches, either," I added. They both paused and watched me as if attempting to read my mind. There really wasn't much to read, at least not anything they didn't already know.

"Or the heartaches. I guess it takes both to create a life worth leading."

I swore I saw the corners of his mouth nudge upward as he spoke. He took a small bite of dessert then leaned forward to scratch his leg.

There was no arguing from my side.

"Good way to put it, Dad." I pointed at him, took the last bite of my dessert, then slid the plate onto the end table. I took it all in: the fire swaying and twirling to its own beat, the nostalgic radio that could have led the song but kept silent, and my parents sitting together on the couch, drunk with contentment.

It suddenly became a fitting end to the evening. I knew there could have been more, but I wanted to be the one to dictate when time was sufficient, not the other way around.

I couldn't help but yawn. "Say... I'm feeling pretty tired. Long day. I'm headin' to bed. See you tomorrow."

"Well, have a good night then." My mom bent her legs and placed her feet on the edge of the coffee table. "I love you, John."

"I love you too, Son." My dad's chin nudged upward, ever so slightly.

I headed up to bed and lay there for quite a while. For some reason, the room felt cold and wintry as if the walls of my room forgot to do their job. I tugged on the blanket and bent my legs in tight.

Of course, I had to check for the Bible in the box. Not sure why I even looked, but for some reason I felt I had to. I guess it gave me proof of where it wasn't and reassurance of where it was. It was gone, but that was fine by me. Bill needed it more than I did.

I soon drifted off, long before I could grasp everything that had happened. It was the most fitful night of sleep I have ever experienced in my life. Somehow, I always know when I toss and turn in my sleep. Sometimes it's glaringly obvious, sometimes not. That particular night, my blanket was kicked aside like it was at fault for something.

So much had happened in so little time. My mind moved from one event to another in rapid-fire fashion, with thoughts so real, so vivid, so lifelike. There were clearly no limits to where they took me. I maneuvered myself around a huge, dimensionless area, but I was clearly the better for it.

I have always been the proud owner of a hyperactive mind, and thoughts can hurt if I'm not careful. My nagging, splitting headache was a not-so-gentle reminder of that. Worst one I ever recall having.

But even through the pain, it all came together like a wonderfully crafted story: the baseball games, the fishing trip, the times with family, and my grandpa heading off to war. Everything. I could feel the muddy ball in my hand, I could smell the aroma of the cake, and I could see the eagle. It was where I needed to be.

Still to this day, I can evoke every detail of that fitful night. The memory of it all is so worth it. I wouldn't trade it for anything.

* * *

The sun peeked over the trees, glaring into my room to convince me to wake up. I rubbed my eyes and stretched out my arms above my head. The loud groan that I made was enough to wake up the neighborhood. I reached up to brush my hair back and instantly caught a dose of reality. The bruise on my temple was still there.

I tilted my head forward, squinted my eyes, and glanced around my bedroom. It was an odd sense of relief as everything looked so pleasantly familiar: the dresser, the carpet, my posters on the wall of vacations and rock bands of the past. And of course, the box. It was even enough to get me to sit up in bed, even though it felt like the first time in quite a while.

I heard noises down the hall and knew right away who it was. She always gets up before I do so she can spend an hour in the bathroom.

I eventually got dressed. No shower needed since I was starving. I could smell breakfast a mile away.

I headed downstairs to the kitchen and found my mom cooking pancakes on the griddle. Sarah had just sat down at the table, pouring a glass of orange juice for herself.

"You want some?" she inquired.

"No, but thanks, Sarah."

"How ya feeling?" she asked just before taking a drink of juice.

"Feeling great, actually. Thanks for asking, Sis. Beautiful morning, eh?" I snatched a plate from the counter, snagged a handful of pancakes, then sat down to eat. They were soon swimming in syrup, just the way I like 'em. Out of the corner of my eye, I could see my sister shaking her head.

My mom had her hand on her hips waiting for the current batch to finish. I continued chatting with Sarah, but sometimes I just know when someone is watching me.

"You look bright and cheery this morning," my mom said in my direction. "Nice to see you up and at 'em. And here I thought you'd be in a lot of pain this morning."

"Yeah, I was out for a long time, wasn't I?" I remarked. "But, you know what? It's great to be back!"

"That's a mild way to put it," my mom said. "Yes, you definitely were out for a while. We were very worried about you, John."

She turned off the griddle and joined us at the table, bringing a platter heaped with a pile of pancakes. I considered just grabbing the whole thing and pouring a tub of syrup over it.

"How much do you remember?" Sarah chimed in.

"Surprisingly, a lot. A whole heck of a lot," I answered then quickly stuffed a forkful in my mouth.

"Like what?" Sarah could tell I was bursting at the seams, and it had nothing to do with all the pancakes I was eating.

"Ah, where to begin..." I paused to finish my humongous bite. "Well, first off I played in that muddy game with Bill. What a hoot! It was the cat's meow if there ever was one..."

"Huh?" Sarah shook her head again. "Anyway, you definitely played in a muddy game. But who's Bill? Is he a new guy on your team?"

"No, no. The other muddy game. You know, the one where Bill slides home in the mud. That game. Well, technically I didn't play... but I was there. I saw the whole darn thing!"

They both let out a quick snicker but kept right on eating.

I dropped my fork and spread out both my hands. "Really! You don't believe me, do you? He was there with all his buddies: Harry, Charlie, and Crazy Eddy. We had such an awesome time hanging out together. We actually got to play a couple of baseball games. 'Course, some things weren't so great, like the..."

They shot me complementary blank stares. I never thought Sarah looked at all like my mom, until then. Her eyes had somehow gotten lighter, her hair darker, and she wasn't smiling, although she looked like she wanted to. The complete silence in the room unnerved me, and it was obvious they didn't believe a word I said.

"By the way, where's Bill?" I asked.

My mom gave me that look from across the table. Her eyes narrowed and could burn my flesh if I didn't resolve it quickly. The same look she used to give me when I was a lot younger and accidentally said a swear word. I hated it back then. It made me feel terrible about something even without her saying a word.

"You mean Grandpa?" she inquired tentatively with her head angled slightly to one side.

"Yeah, of course, Grandpa. How's the old man doin'?"

I watched them exchange glances, and quickly realized questions aren't always answered with words. My mom slowly placed her fork next to her plate and folded her hands, her elbows rested gently on the table. She leaned forward toward me, her motherly posture evident.

"John..." she started.

I really disliked it when she did that. I felt like I was twelve again and she was about to explain something I already knew. Only this time, I didn't.

"Yes..." I said in a slow, rolling fashion.

I could tell right away she didn't appreciate my smart-aleck attitude. And I felt bad as that was not my intention. I tried sitting more upright to offset my words. I smiled at her, but it was not returned.

"John, he took a hard fall, and I think it shook him up a bit. He hasn't been out of his bed since. He's been resting a lot, but he's still in a lot of pain."

It felt like I was hit in the head with that godforsaken baseball all over again. I had hoped I would never have to relive that pain, the distinct feeling of blunt trauma. But the abruptness of the news felt eerily similar. I wanted to jump up and run but couldn't move. I wanted to scream, but felt nobody would hear me anyway. I'm normally not one to gasp when surprised as it seems like such a sign of weakness to me. But sometimes I can't stop myself.

"Sorry, I thought you knew," she added.

"How would I know? He was fine last time I saw him..."

"He fell right after you left for your game," Sarah added. "He was heading back to his room when I heard a loud thud in the hallway. I went to see what was wrong when I found him."

"Did you take him to the hospital? I mean, I'm sure they can fix him up there."

My mom twitched her nose as she looked over at my sister. Sarah only turned to look out the window. It was clearly not the first time my mom had pondered the thought, nor the last.

"The paramedics came, helped him recover and lie in bed," she explained. "They gave him a few things to calm him and slow down his rapid breathing, plus a few things for pain. They suggested we keep a close eye on him here."

"And they can do that at the damn hospital! I don't understand why we don't take him in, I mean..."

"John, it's what he wanted." She hesitated, watching my lack of movement. "They asked him, and he said no to the hospital. He said he wanted to be here with us."

I threw my napkin on top of my plate, covering the remaining syrup-soaked pancakes. Anger directed at no one seemed wasteful to me, but I didn't know how else to feel.

I glanced around the room and noticed the little things that had changed since I last set foot in that kitchen. The sunflowers on the drapes above the sink stood out to me first. Not sure if I ever noticed those before. The cupboards had been updated long ago to a light maple finish, and I remembered when we painted the room a faint yellow. Our old appliances, especially the refrigerator, suddenly looked so new. And so large.

But I couldn't get past the dreariness of the room. I looked around for the source of what I felt but didn't see it. I sniffed but didn't smell it. With darkness being the absence of light, I knew I would never find its origin. It wasn't really there, yet I knew it was. I had to look.

I glared at my mom and realized what I had to do.

"I'd like to go see him," I declared. My mom was taken aback by my bluntness. So was I.

"You're certainly welcome to see him, John," she said. "But he does need his sleep. Later today might be better..."

I barely heard her trailing comments as I walked away down the hall.

Chapter 22

The hallway appeared to be the one place in the house where the bright sunshine had not penetrated. The hollow, damp feeling was inescapable. It was still decorated with many candid pictures and family portraits, but it looked strikingly different. While the black and white pictures suddenly appeared more vibrant and real, the color ones had faded to become almost unrecognizable.

I certainly appreciated where I had been, but I didn't much care for where that hall was taking me. No familiarity, no intimacy. Unfortunately, it only went one way.

I stopped at the doorway to my grandpa's room and figured out how one could get lost in such darkness. Blankets concealed the windows and were clearly put there for a reason. But I wasn't sure if it kept something in or out. I decided not to flip the switch for fear the light would usher in reality.

His door was slightly ajar, so I pushed it ever so slowly to minimize the noise. I tiptoed in and approached the end of his bed. I stood there, concentrating on his rhythmic breathing, hoping to resonate with his lifeblood. It was clear that a new point had been reached, and my desire was greater than his ability.

A part of me thought I had exhausted his stories, that I had gotten my fill. But I became selfish. There were more I had to get out of him.

I walked over to the side of his bed. He stirred with a pronounced tremor, slowly opened his eyes, then surveyed his surroundings. I looked into the hollowness of his moist eyes and saw a damp cavern storing scrolls of parchment, each containing something legendary. The rest of his gaunt face, however, told a much different story, one that I didn't care to hear or experience.

He angled his head, then suddenly gave a startled look in my direction. As soon as he realized it was me, his posture eased and a smile overcome his expression. He attempted to maneuver himself upright but quickly learned he couldn't do it on his own. I reached over and grabbed his arm to help him up. The thinness and coldness of his skin startled me, but I was also surprised by its reassuring softness.

"Hey Grandpa, how ya doin'?" I asked hopefully loud enough for him to hear.

He shifted in his bed and suddenly grimaced with a quick-and-dirty pain. He quickly gazed over in my direction with wide-open eyes.

"Compared to what?" he responded with an unexpected yet recognizable wit. He had a point there.

"I... don't know. I never thought about that." I had to smile at that one. "Compared to yesterday, I guess."

"Well, about the same then. Compared to sixty years ago, not so good." He tried to smile but just couldn't. Hopefully, his joy was only lost and not stolen.

I watched him then decided to jump right into it. "I wanted to ask you something, Grandpa. When did you and Grandma start dating?"

It was, surprisingly, a story I had never heard.

His eyebrows raised, and he shook his head in a show of intrigue.

"Come, sit over here, John." He patted the side of his bed.

As I cautiously sat down next to him, I was hit with an overwhelming antiseptic smell. I almost gagged. I could also tell it was purposely covering up a pronounced odor, one that told me he was no longer in control.

"Well, being the looker that I was..." he started his story.

He attempted to couple it with laughter, but it forced him to erupt into a pronounced but short coughing fit. He covered his mouth which helped it stop, at least temporarily.

"Why do you speak in past tense?" I shot him a grin he subsequently returned.

"So, I was playin' basketball when we met. Actually, she liked to say we met again for the first time. Sure, we knew each other from school and activities around town, but we didn't start dating until much later.

"Odd that it was basketball 'cause I don't recall playing much except for only a few seasons. Wasn't my sport. Anyway. Most of the details from the game escape me, but I do remember going after a loose ball at half court."

He unleashed another loud, deep cough, then quickly continued.

"This part, I clearly remember. I was running pretty hard to grab it, battling step for step with one of the jerks from the other team. I reached out and grabbed the ball with my fingertips, barely enough to throw it back into play."

"Was she one of the cheerleaders rootin' ya on?" I asked.

"No no, not at all. She was the helpless girl sitting in the front row I unexpectedly landed on when I couldn't stop myself!"

"Oh my goodness! Really? That's hilarious!"

"Yeah, poor girl... I was never one to do anything half-assed, so I landed pretty hard. I... I was probably sweating like a pig."

His body shook like something had just escaped, something that had laid dormant for a long time.

"Doesn't sound like the best of beginnings," I admitted, a bit puzzled. "I assume you eventually asked her out then? She forgave you for... dropping by?"

"Yeah, I did ask her out. Don't know if she ever forgave me, though. She was clearly not blessed with very good eyesight as I approached her after the game and she seemed delighted to see me. We hit it off, so I decided to ask her out."

"You... big stud, you."

"Yeah maybe I was. But I sure was comin' off a tough time. I had just come back from that stupid war, and I wasn't really lookin' to be honest. Don't know if she was, but I guess opportunity just fell right in her lap! If that's what you wanna call me..."

We both chuckled, but I tried my best to keep it subdued so he wouldn't have another coughing fit. I hated to have to do that. He appeared to be consumed by pain like something was eating away at him from the inside out. I briefly looked away.

"I still hadn't gotten over Anna. But at least I came back to playing baseball again."

I instantly stopped laughing and snapped a look directly at him. Did he just say what I thought he said? I glared directly into his eyes, and him at me. I cannot put into words all of the emotions that came boiling up at that moment, but surprise and happiness were two of them.

I squinted until one eye closed just slightly. But somehow, my view had become much clearer. He had never told me that story before, the story about Anna and the ring. Nor had he ever told me he quit baseball. But the reality of it was that it was reality.

He put his hand on my back, which further startled me. I guess he felt it necessary to complete the transfer, as if the warm dampness of the air was thick enough to get in the way.

I decided to match his directness. "So... when did you two go ice skating?"

"On our first date. Over at Greenfield Park on the frozen lake. It was always bumpy as shallow lakes tend to be when they freeze. But boy did we have fun."

"I bet you did, Bill. I bet you did."

"I only fell on my butt three times, so maybe she was impressed with my athletic prowess."

"No doubt. I'm sure she was."

I leaned my hip to one side and stretched out my leg so I could dig deep into my pocket. I found it, took it out, and raised it in the air close enough for him to see it clearly. He instantly knew what it was. When I grabbed it out of the box, it made the inside look so vast, so deep, so hollow. But it was well worth sharing.

"Is this a ticket from your skating?" I asked proudly.

Color returned to his cheeks as if a warmer blood started flowing.

"Why yes it is." He slowly reached out and grabbed the frayed ticket. I inserted it into his shaking hand, and he squeezed his fingers just enough to hold it.

Funny how memory works. A skating ticket from six decades ago was instantly recognizable. If I asked him what he had for breakfast that morning, however, he would have no clue. As if the past was nearer and closer than the present.

He inspected it closely by twisting his wrist, just enough to see both the front and the back. It had turned a dull yellowish brown, and one of the corners had ripped off. There were noticeable indentations on both edges, and I could faintly read the lettering on the front that spelled out 'Greenfield Park.'

I was looking so intently at the ticket that I barely caught sight of the tears that landed on the soft pillow. He flipped the ticket over and squinted intently.

"Yup, that's my writin' on the back."

"Where?"

I snapped my head and hunched down toward the bed to get a closer look at the back of the raggedy, old ticket. Sure enough, there it was. For some reason, I had never looked at the back before.

It read "February 23, 1946... Bill + Arlis" in faint black letters.

Arlis. I'll never forget a name like that.

I looked up at the ceiling, hoping that would contain my emotions. But it was hopeless. I still think about my grandma all the time, especially after our double date so long ago. Yet, it felt like only yesterday. That was a special evening, but it had nothing to do with the skills of our dancing or the deliciousness of the sodas at the malt shop. To have that one last moment of time to share with her – and my grandpa – was beyond priceless.

I knew they would get together. I guess sometimes knowledge is a good thing.

"John, you should let him get some rest. It's been a long day."

Her voice startled me as I had no clue she was standing in the doorway. I quickly wiped my eyes and looked up at my mom.

She was right, even if I didn't want to admit it.

"I should go, Grandpa. Too much stuff to do."

I turned to look at him, but he had already fallen asleep. I inspected him, watching his chest go up and down, just to be sure. I glanced around, but the ticket was nowhere to be found. I leaned over to look all around the sheets and comforter. I stooped down low around the edges of the bed, and down by the end table. I even got down on my knees to look. It was gone.

"Whatcha looking for, John?"

"Ah... it was nothing, nothing at all." I stood upright and walked toward the door.

I'm not sure why, but I decided not to tell her. Too difficult to explain. Clinging to it tightly might compel me to remember it forever.

I followed my mom down the dimly lit hall. As a kid, I loved to run up and down that hallway, making noises that would startle a mouse. Sarah and I used it as a bowling alley for a while, pins flying haphazardly as we threw yet another strike. It was where I perfected my bowling skills, even though I was only eight at the time.

I'm certain I was insensitive to all the pictures on the walls, who was in them and what they meant. But suddenly I admired that hallway. Perhaps it was a two-way street. Or better yet, perhaps it was not merely a portal but a destination in and of itself.

My mom was surprisingly quiet as we walked.

"How much longer does he have, Mom?" I asked.

She stopped walking and I could see the strain on her face. I'm certain she was trying to figure out what to tell me.

"I'm not sure, John, not sure. He hasn't been awake for some time now."

I looked over at her and wanted to tell her she was wrong. But I decided to let it go.

"Hmm, I was just showing him how to throw a knuckleball."

She laughed, "He would have appreciated that. Grandpa and his sports... he's always loved 'em."

"Something I've always appreciated about him, even if I didn't always listen to his stories," I reasoned then paused to change the subject. "Say, you sure we shouldn't consider taking him to a hospital?"

"John!" It was a harsh, tainted way of saying my name. "What would that do? Prolong his life for how much longer? He's 81, John."

"I was just asking, Mom. Just asking..." I extended my open hands.

I tried to act calm, but somehow a frustration boiled up inside me. At that stage, I was not one to relinquish control very easily.

She looked down, sniffed, and rubbed her cheek. She continued, but this time more subdued, "He's lived a very full life. If you're going to cling to anything, John, hold onto that assurance."

I scratched my head, then decided to walk away, more briskly than I anticipated.

"John, I'm sure you understand..." I heard my mom's trailing voice behind me.

I actually did understand, but understanding and agreeing are two different things. My selfishness was getting the best of me. At the time, I didn't realize mine was not the only opinion to consider.

I wasn't mad... or maybe I was. Dammit, I didn't know. I had so many emotions, and they all ran together into one jumbled mess. I always admired my mom and sister as they were more comfortable with expressing themselves. Granted their cup runneth over sometimes, but at least they sat down at the table to drink. My cup never usually left the cupboard.

I headed for my room simply because I didn't know where else to go. I jumped on my bed, flipped over on my back, and put my hands behind my head.

I closed my eyes thinking of everything that had happened lately. As the memories swirled in my head, I had a distinct realization that brought more questions than answers. Why is it that memories from the past become better over time? Was it a time-consuming maturing process, necessary for understanding? Or it was a farsightedness I was unaware I had, where clarity only came from distance. Either way, my current state of affairs was forever hopeless. My present felt like a tarnished version of my past.

I opened my eyes, glanced around, and began to focus on the box. It was sitting on my dresser right where I left it. I questioned if the contents were still there, even though I had made up my mind on their whereabouts.

I jumped out of bed and grabbed the box from my dresser. It was the most tattered and worn it had ever looked. I swore the rust was eating away at the hinges and they'd fall off any day now.

I placed it on my bed and sat down next to it. I purposely opened it slowly as I had somehow grown fond of the creaking sound. Just as I suspected, only one item remained, and I wondered how much longer the feather had left before it disappeared. Certainly, there were still small scraps of dirt scattered throughout the bottom, remnants of that muddy ball. Someday, I'd clean it out. As I suspected, the ticket was gone.

When I first received the box, it looked so small, so full of unimportance. But it grew in size. The small, white feather was dwarfed by the enormity of the box. It wasn't until years later did I realize there was actually a vast amount of contents in that box. The type of contents that never disappear and can never be taken away from me. Priceless contents that I can take with me wherever I go. Memories from the past that I so richly experienced.

As I sat there, I realized I should ask him where the box came from and why he gave it to me. The last and suddenly most important story that I wanted to hear. But my mom was right, he needed his sleep.

I also knew I had stuff to do and a few errands to run before I headed out. It had been so long since I had seen my buddy, Caleb. I had so much to tell him.

Chapter 23

I woke up as groggy as ever. My eyes felt like they were sewn shut, and my whole body felt bruised and beaten. As I tried to stir, I quickly realized I had stayed out way too late the night before. It was great hanging out with Caleb again, don't get me wrong, but we should have called it a night hours earlier.

It only took one hurried glance into the mirror to convince myself to take a shower. It was a Tuesday morning, and I was surprised I hadn't heard anyone wake up yet and head to school or work. I enjoyed my long, hot shower and headed downstairs. At least I felt somewhat awake.

As I shuffled through the cupboards to find my favorite cereal, I heard an unfamiliar voice inside our house. High and soft yet raspy. Definitely an older woman. I gave myself a quick inspection, happy I had chosen a clean T-shirt. The commotion was definitely coming from down the hall, so I headed there to investigate.

As I approached the back room, the voice became clearer and more refined, and she was conversing with my mother. A back and forth discussion in hushed tones, like they were agreeing on the strands of their secret. I arrived at the doorway and was shocked to find Sarah leaning against the closet, arms folded tightly, and staring down at one of the tinged floorboards. She was still wearing her polar bear pajamas.

I sniffed a few times, my head moving back and forth as I suddenly noticed a pronounced sterile odor that added a warmth to the air. Even worse than the day before.

"What's going on?" I was utterly confused. "And why aren't you at school, Sarah?"

I looked over at her, but she did not return my gaze. She barely acknowledged me, yet her posture did not portray rudeness. My mom turned around with a smooth motion like she was expecting to see me. She was nicely dressed like she was heading to work, her arms working in unison so she could rest her chin on her hand. Yet she bore a noticeably fraught anxiety on her face. She glanced at the visitor, then quickly back at me.

"John, this is Ms. Sanford. She's from Hospice Care." She hesitated to complete her thought. "She's going to be with us today."

"You can call me Rose," she added with a sympathetic smile. I ignored her outstretched hand.

"Why is she here?" I snapped.

"You can at least say 'hi,' John," my mom scolded. "She's here to help Grandpa."

I don't know why I even asked as I knew what it meant. I was familiar with the implications, whether I liked them or not. Did I not know what else to say? I was afraid to ask the real questions that needed to be asked. Or worse yet, afraid to learn the answers.

"I'm sorry. Nice to meet you." I ceremoniously shook her hand. "But I just talked to him yesterday so I don't see why..."

I looked over at Bill and instantly saw the motivation. Nighttime had been a cruel visitor. His skin was colorless and dull like the ashen remains of an extinguished campfire. His breathing, heavy and labored. He tossed and turned in between each breath like he had an awful itch that he couldn't scratch. He had clearly moved on to a different place, even though he still lay in his bed.

"Come in, John," said Ms. Sanford as she walked past me through the doorway. "I'll be right back."

I scrunched my nose and shook my head quickly from side to side. Easy for her to be so nonchalant, I thought, she had been through this before.

I stood in the doorway, not knowing where else to go. Sarah was nearby but only there physically, and my mom moved next to the bed watching her father. She sat down on the lone chair. The sounds of his dense breathing were difficult to ignore. It was the first time in our lives when the three of us were in the same room with nothing to talk about.

I heard a clanking in the kitchen and turned around to catch Ms. Sanford coming down the hall. I briefly glanced up, looked straight into her reassuring eyes, and instantly felt horrible for my thoughts and actions.

"Excuse me, John," she whispered as she passed. "Why don't you guys get more comfortable?"

I shuffled to the side as she walked past with a chair she had grabbed from the kitchen. She made another trip for a second chair and placed them next to my mother by the bed. I sat down in the middle while Sarah continue standing, still leaning against the closet door. She refused to get any closer.

We watched him struggle with every gasp of air, every movement. His motions were similar to those of a slow-motion, prize fighter pushing away his competitor. The defensiveness, the reluctant hand-to-hand combat with someone or something I couldn't see. But his competition had clearly snatched control. The pain in his face was evident as a grimace accompanied every breath.

I leaned forward to hear his voice but couldn't make out what he was saying. The look my mom gave me told me she too had become curious. The flow of guttural noises and random words were from someone who was clearly having a really bad dream.

It could very well have been me.

My mom grabbed a few pillows from the closet with Rose helping her. They placed them by his side and nudged them close to provide at least one source of comfort for him.

Rose stood right behind us and began singing a quiet, soft hymn. I didn't recognize it, but it sure was pretty. Her voice became smooth and lyrical as if the song became a polish for the scuffs created by time. Bill instantly responded with a slower, more pronounced breathing. Must have been a song he knew.

I was calmed by her singing, yet I could not avoid sudden urges of queasiness. My stomach tossed and turned almost in unison with Bill's jerky movements. How could I like something yet feel physically ill at the same time? It was a mix of senses I would not recommend for the faint of heart.

I had an overwhelming urge to run out of the room, but my intuitive mother reached over and grabbed my arm right as I was about to stand up. Her hand was warm, but I felt guilty I did not reciprocate. Shouldn't I have been providing comfort for her?

Something suddenly changed. Bill's motions became smooth and rhythmic and his voice more pronounced. He was no longer a boxer but more a ballet dancer. It was clear he had stopped fighting, but whether he had won or lost, I wasn't quite sure.

"Oh my goodness. He looks like he's walking, Mom," I pointed out.

Even Sarah acknowledged it from behind. His arms started reaching out almost like someone was greeting him. His voice also became louder and his words more discernible.

"I think he's trying to say something, Mom," said Sarah who was becoming more intrigued but had still not moved any closer.

I sat back in my chair and closed my eyes, trying to stop the room from its never-ending tailspin. I listened intently to his speech and it forced my mind to wander. As I began to focus, my thoughts provided context for his words.

Oddly enough, it was a trick that Caleb taught me when trying to recognize voices in animated movies. I close my eyes in order to focus my thoughts. Removing the things that don't really matter, like space and time. Then it became clear. I saw and heard what I really needed.

I thought of his past, the past that I knew, the past that I lived in. It became a convoluted movie in fast forward, and I had no control to slow it down. I could see us playing baseball out by Boomer's mill; all the guys were there. We ran toward the lake but then suddenly jumped onto a boat, and there we were fishing. I looked up to the tallest tree by the lake and saw planes flying overhead and bombs dropping toward us. We ran for cover behind a grove of bushes and suddenly came upon a large dinner table. I immediately sat down.

My body shook in a startled fashion as I smelled a familiar scent. I instinctively shifted my tongue around, almost licking my lips. I swallowed hard and suddenly perceived something delicious in my mouth. It was clearly the flavor of vanilla pudding cake.

I listened closer to Bill's words and instantly realized what he was saying. Or I should say to whom.

I glanced around the table and his entire family was there. His parents, his sisters, and his brother, Donny. They were all enjoying their cake, laughing and talking like there was no tomorrow. But they each listened intently above the laughter as each in turn acknowledged Bill's distant voice as he called out their names.

I looked up and watched him enter the dining room through the arched doorway. How did I not notice he wasn't there? Everyone jumped out of their seats to meet Bill, ecstatic to see someone they hadn't seen in a very long time. I had a unique view in watching it all. Almost as if I was there.

"He looks so peaceful now, Mom," I heard Sarah say, her voice now much closer. My eyes opened slowly.

Almost in synchronization, Rose opened her Bible and began reading 2 Corinthians 4:16-18: "So we do not lose heart. Though our outer self is wasting away, our inner self is being renewed day by day. For this light momentary affliction is preparing for us an eternal weight of glory beyond all comparison, as we look not to the things that are seen but to the things that are unseen. For the things that are seen are transient, but the things that are unseen are eternal."

As soon as I heard the words, I knew they sounded familiar. I closed my eyes again as I realized where and when I had heard them before. That little boy was now running around without a worry to be had. His deep dark eyes complemented his toothy grin and nicely reflected his happy and carefree attitude.

From the table, I watched him rush through an open field that stretched to eternity. It was full of tall, auburn grass that did nothing to impede his ability to run.

His destination was clearly a large house far off on a small hill. As he finally approached it, I watched intently as he walked up the steps to the large, white front porch. He put his hand on the railing, and then turned to wave goodbye. Before I knew it, he had dashed through the front door and was gone. I breathed a sigh of relief as I was certain he had finally made it home.

The room became silent. The finality of it compelled us all to sit motionless for a brief moment in time. Rose placed her hand on my mom's shoulder and whispered, "I'm sorry." I glanced over at my mom and sister, partly to see their reactions. My arms wrapped themselves around my mother. I hadn't heard her cry in a long time, but I will always recall the muted sobbing against my chest. My hug became even tighter, even closer.

I walked over to Sarah and hugged her as securely as I could. At first, her arms were caught between us as she covered her mouth. But she soon slipped them out and wrapped them around my back. She wiped her eyes on my shoulder as we embraced for longer than we ever had before.

Chapter 24

The day finally arrived. All the preparation had hopefully been completed. Everything from the choice of flower bouquets to the old pictures and family portraits to place on the back table. The hallway was empty.

My mom made most of the phone calls, but Sarah and I helped out where we could. Whether or not we were ready, it was going to happen. As Bill would have said, 'There goes nothing.'

But this was something. This was something that meant a lot to me, actually. I didn't think I could ever be fully prepared for when death stole a loved one from me. I knew it was going to happen at some point. But it was still a deep-down hurt that would take a long time to heal.

"Time to go, Sarah. We're gonna be late," my mom yelled up the stairs.

The car was fully packed, I made sure of that. We had everything we needed, from flowers to cards to boxes of pictures. The car had been running for ten minutes, and my mom and I were getting impatient.

I slid my finger under my annoying necktie for the hundredth time.

"I'm coming, I'm coming," answered Sarah as she ran down the stairs. She wore a navy dress covered with a thin, white sweater and her long hair was put up in a way she had never done before. I distinctly remember how beautiful she looked that day.

The funeral was not as packed as I thought it would be. Certainly, Bill never met anyone he didn't call a friend. However, he managed to outlive many of them. All of his baseball and wartime buddies were long gone, but of course, never to be forgotten.

Right before it was to begin, I peeked in to watch people taking their seats. Even from way in the back, I could smell the fresh fragrance of the flowers. Roses, carnations, lilies.

I looked up in front and saw the signal. It was time.

The pastor called us into the large, well-lit room for one last viewing before the casket was to be closed. There were wooden chairs on both sides of the room with an aisle down the middle. Most of the back ones were empty. I could feel all eyes penetrate on us as we walked up to the front. Sarah went first, bending over slightly to kiss his hand. She went straight to her nearby seat.

Then it was my turn. I had thought for a long time what I wanted to do. Ultimately, I decided on what was the most meaningful to me, and to him as well. I grabbed what I wanted out of my pocket and placed it in the left breast pocket of his jacket. It stuck out just a bit, looking to me like a classy white handkerchief. I took a quick glance at the pure, white feather, looked at him hoping for one final wink, then said goodbye for the last time.

It took me a while to figure out why the feather stayed while the others disappeared. It had appeared before me in a way that some people might have missed, and it stayed with me wherever I went. Certainly, we all have one. An uninterrupted continuity across everything we do. We just have to decide how we want to share it with others. Believe me, it is well worth sharing.

While I will make sure my memory of that feather lasts forever, in the end it was indeed his. His story.

I reached back and grabbed my mom's hand. She told me the day before this was the moment she dreaded. She had never been one who enjoyed goodbyes. She said something very quietly to him and kissed him on the cheek. One last time.

I continued holding her hand as we sat down. We watched the flag being draped on top. As precisely as possible.

Knowing who he was, my mom had decided to have an open mike for anyone to come up and tell a story about Bill. There was a pause in the quiet room, but I somehow found the courage to go first. I stood before the group, concentrating on what I wanted to say and avoided thinking about what I didn't want to do.

"I have so many wonderful memories of my grandpa. Some I can tell in public, and some I probably shouldn't," I reckoned, then waited for the laughter to subside. "I guess what I appreciated most about him was his raw sense of humor. One night, we were eating dinner outside on our patio, and he was in the middle of one of his long-winded stories.

"Meanwhile, he continued gnawing on an apparently under-cooked carrot. Difficult to chew, I'm sure, when you don't have any teeth. In the middle of his story, he picked the carrot out of his mouth and threw it pretty far on the ground. Of course, he kept right on talking like nothing happened."

I paused and looked back at the table of pictures. I shook my head and joined in the laughter.

"I'll really miss him," I added.

I glanced at my mom as I sat back down and gave her a wink.

Other stories were shared, from old neighbors to friends from long ago. Ms. Benning, his neighbor from forty years ago, told a hilarious story about the time Bill convinced her to view some rare, red bats under a shrouded cage he kept in his house. She lifted up the sheet then jumped and screamed hysterically when he simultaneously yelled 'boo.' Of course, they were bats, but the baseball kind hanging from a wire and painted red.

I unleashed the loudest laugh I had in a while, only to be drowned out by others.

And from that point on, we all joined in a throng of laughter after each story. Some might have considered that inappropriate for a funeral, but they didn't know Bill.

As I listened, though, I realized it was not the content of the stories that mattered. Once we all grew into celebratory moods, we could have told anything and gotten a laugh. My eyes watered from laughing so hard.

But nothing could have prepared me for the last and final story. A story I had not heard but had so much desire to hear.

It was told by my mom.

As she stepped out of her chair, I recall glancing over and being shocked she would consider saying anything. I felt my eyes moisten even more, this time out of pure empathy. I knew this was difficult for her. She stood upright behind the podium and placed her hands on top. She appeared to focus on the back table as she spoke.

"It is so wonderful to see all of you and to hear your wonderful stories. I wouldn't be surprised if my dad is joining us in our laughter. We clearly all enjoyed his quick wit and, uh... boisterous storytelling. I also treasured his love and compassion for others."

She stopped to gather her thoughts.

"This especially showed as I watched him care so much for my children. He was there for them in so many ways."

I raised my head quickly. My heart pounded but my breathing stopped. Wherever she was going with this story, I deeply desired to go with her.

"One of my favorite stories was from when John and Sarah were very young." She glanced over to us with a soothing warmth. I stared intently. "They had this long phase of playing a game I affectionately called 'pirate and damsel.'

They would search the house for random treasures then throw them into a box. Well, back when my dad could move around better, he would get down on his hands and knees and join them. I hope they never made him walk the plank!

"At the time, they used a cardboard box to store everything as that was all we could afford at the time. My dad wanted them to have a proper place to store their loot, so for Christmas that year he got them a wonderful, new treasure chest. I don't know where he bought it, but it was a beautiful box they used for a very long time.

"While their game was soon forgotten, I love what that chest of treasures signifies to me," she looked down but then glanced up directly at me. "And I was so happy to see it out again recently."

She walked back to her seat and instantly put her soft hand on my shaking back. I remember being proud of her as she kept her composure so well.

I thought of all the wonderful stories and memories of my grandfather. They were all unleashed at once, and I could still see his smiling face laughing and talking like there wasn't a care in the world. And I suspect all of that is still true today.

My fond memories of the tattered box also came rushing back. We did store our treasures there. I was mad at myself for long ago tossing it aside, but apparently it needed to be discarded in order for me to find it again.

Our pirate and damsel games seemed like only yesterday, but somehow I had completely forgotten about the box. I thought it looked vaguely familiar back when he first brought it out and set it on the kitchen table. But I said nothing about it. I suspected somewhere in my mind, I knew.

"Thank you," I whispered to my mom. It was all I could say.

* * *

We drove in a large caravan to the cemetery. It was a long drive but worth the effort for Bill to be buried with full military honors. He would also be right next to my grandma. She had served in the army during the war, not surprising for the warden. The cemetery had kept a site open just for Bill. The blank tombstone near Grandma that confused me as a kid now suddenly made sense.

We were completely quiet on the way there. I can't say enjoyment is the right word, but we certainly appreciated every aspect of the funeral. I'm not sure if we knew what we wanted, but it turned out to be just what we were looking for.

We took a back road to the cemetery so our long line of slow-moving vehicles could avoid the busy highway. I admired the beautiful rows of trees that stood at attention as we passed. Oaks, maples, and birch, all awaiting our arrival.

The 21-gun salute was impressive. Even though we knew it was coming, it startled Sarah and me on every shot. My mom sat motionless as she had clearly been through this before. She knew what to expect, but that didn't make it any easier. As I held her hand, I could sense she was in deep thought, most likely relishing another story from the past.

We took the same route back as I had enjoyed the tree-lined road. As we approached the last segment before turning onto the busy highway, I saw it up in the tree. It was as beautiful and majestic as ever, standing guard like a sentry guarding his lair. The eagle barely moved but clearly acknowledged our presence. He watched us with a focused intensity. But his protective stance was for a different reason as the nest behind him was empty.

I pulled the car off onto the dusty shoulder as I wanted to stay long enough to appreciate the scene. That was when I spotted it. Scattered amongst the leaves and sticks underneath the large oak. I quickly opened the car door and ran over to pick up the feather. It looked vaguely familiar yet different in its own unique way. Most importantly, however, the tip on the hollow quill was broken and sharp, providing a reservoir for the requisite ink that has flowed ever since I found my voice.

* * *

I kept that box close to me over the years, always taking it with me wherever I went. At first, others asked me about the emptiness of it. 'Such a large box to hold a single, ordinary feather,' someone said to me once. But I knew better.

I finally opened up about my time spent with Bill. My mom and sister were amazed at my experience and relished that time to listen and take it all in. I told others, of course, but they didn't understand. I suspect they were concerned about my sanity, or lack thereof, but that had nothing to do with the box.

The box filled over the years, with many old and new treasures alike. But before I filled it with my own items, I made certain they all came back, everything came back just as I remembered them.

And the day my son asked me where the muddy ball came from was the day I started writing this story.

About the Author

Paul Schumacher lives in Colorado with his amazing wife, three wonderful kids, and two lazy cats. He works by day as an engineer and fits in writing whenever he can. *The Tattered Box* is his first novel. You can talk to him on Twitter at @pgschuey.

37866000130095

CPSIA information can be obtained
at www.ICGtesting.com
Printed in the USA
FSOW02n0918200117
29865FS